"Any woman can sh... you," Olivia said, her tone dismissive. **"Very few have the benefit of royal training."**

Tarek's expression barely changed, a flicker in his eyes that was nearly imperceptible. "You think I might find value in that?"

"Unless you want the country you've spent so much of your life protecting to burn, I think you will. There is an entirely different manner of strength that is coveted in politics."

"I don't have to marry you to receive the benefit of your training."

"It's true. You don't. And perhaps that's a good place for us to start."

"I can promise you a marriage between the two of us would be nothing like the one you shared with your first husband."

She didn't doubt it.

"Give me one month. I will help you with the finer points, and we can engage in a kind of courtship. A bit of something for the media, something for your people. If it doesn't work out, there is no harm. But if it does..."

He stood abruptly, his movements fluid. It reminded her of the strike of a viper. So still in the moment just before the fatal hit was administered. Over before you ever knew it had occurred.

"Dowager Queen Olivia of Alansund, we have an accord. You have thirty days to convince me that you are indispensable. If you are successful, I will make you my wife."

Maisey Yates is a *USA TODAY* bestselling author of more than thirty romance novels. She has a coffee habit she has no interest in kicking, and a slight Pinterest addiction. She lives with her husband and children in the Pacific Northwest. When Maisey isn't writing she can be found singing in the grocery store, shopping for shoes online and probably not doing dishes. Check out her website, maiseyyates.com.

Books by Maisey Yates

Harlequin Presents

His Diamond of Convenience
To Defy a Sheikh
One Night to Risk It All
Forged in the Desert Heat
His Ring Is Not Enough
The Couple who Fooled the World
A Game of Vows

The Chatsfield

Sheikh's Desert Duty

One Night With Consequences

Married for Amari's Heir

The Call of Duty

A Royal World Apart
At His Majesty's Request
Pretender to the Throne

Secret Heirs of Powerful Men

Heir to a Desert Legacy
Heir to a Dark Inheritance

Visit the Author Profile page
at Harlequin.com for more titles.

Maisey Yates

Bound to the Warrior King

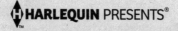
HARLEQUIN PRESENTS®

Recycling programs
for this product may
not exist in your area.

ISBN-13: 978-0-373-13368-0

Bound to the Warrior King

First North American Publication 2015

Copyright © 2015 by Maisey Yates

Printed in U.S.A.

Bound to the Warrior King

Elyse and Elizabeth, I blame you for this book...
I mean, I thank you for this book.
It was as fun as I thought it would be.

CHAPTER ONE

SHE WAS FRAIL. And pale. Her blond hair pulled back into a tight and elegant bun, the long sleeves of her dress and the hem that brushed the floor were likely an attempt at sparing her European skin from the full brunt of the Taharan sun.

It would not do. A few moments out in the environment he'd spent his past decade in and she would perish.

Nothing more than a white lily drying on the sand until she returned back to the dust, sent away on the next dry, hot breeze.

Whatever advisor had imagined she would make a suitable wife for the Sheikh of Tahar was clearly yet another man he needed to have removed from his position.

When it came to his staff, Tarek's needs were not Malik's. As was becoming clearer and clearer every day.

A political alliance. That was what this potential marriage had been called. As Tarek knew nothing of politics he'd been more than willing to investigate the possibilities of the union.

But no. Seeing her now... It would not stand.

"Take her away from my sight," Tarek said.

She looked up, her expression smooth yet shot through with steel. "No."

He arched a brow. "No?"

"I cannot leave here."

"Certainly you can. The same way you came in." It was

he who could not leave. He who could not go back and seek the solace of the desert.

He, who had been kept in isolation for most of his life, who now had to find a way to rule a population of millions.

She tilted her chin upward and he could see her regal bearing, the aristocratic lines of her profile. And he realized he had not bothered to hold on to her name.

He was certain he had been told when, two weeks previously, he'd been informed a princess from a European kingdom would be coming to offer herself in marriage. And yet, his brain had sifted through and retained some things, but not others.

Her name was not essential, and therefore it had been dropped.

"You do not understand, my sheikh," she continued, her voice steady, echoing in the vast throne room.

He rather liked this room. It was very like a cave.

"Do I not?" he asked, still unaccustomed to the title.

"No. I cannot return to Alansund without this union secured. In fact, it would be best if I did not return at all."

"And why is that?"

"There is no place for me. I am not born of royalty. I am not even native to the country."

"Are you not?"

"I'm American," she said. "I met my husband...my late husband, the king, when he was at school. Now he is dead. His brother is in his place, and is set on taking a wife. One who isn't me, thank God. But he has determined my value is in a dynastic marriage abroad. And so...here I am."

"Your name," he said, because he was tired of not knowing it.

She blinked. "You do not know my name?"

"I have no time for trivialities, and as I am not keeping you, your name did not seem important. However, now I will have it."

She tilted her chin upward, her expression haughty. "Forgive me, your highness, but my name is not considered a triviality in most settings. I'm Dowager Queen Olivia of Alansund. And I had thought we were going to discuss the merits of marriage."

Tarek shifted in his seat, lifting his hand and smoothing his beard. "I am not entirely certain there is any merit to marriage."

She blinked her large luminous blue eyes. "Then, why am I here?"

"My advisors felt that it would be beneficial for me to speak to you. I am not certain."

"Is there another woman you prefer?"

He wasn't certain how to answer the question. Because it was a foreign thought. Women had never been a part of his life. Of his exile. "No. Why do you ask?"

"You do require an heir, I would assume."

She was not wrong in that. He was the last of the al-Khalij family. All that remained of a once-mighty bloodline. Curse his brother for not taking a bride. For not procreating when he had the chance. Now it would fall to Tarek, and nothing in his life had prepared him for the task. Quite the contrary, he had been told that family would be nothing more than a weakness to one such as him. He had been trained to cast off the lusts of the flesh. In order to protect his country he'd had to become something more than a man. He'd had to become a part of the rock that grew out of the dry, impassable desert. Asking him to become blood and bone again was a tall order.

But now he was all that stood between Tahar and her enemies. All that stood between his nation and ruin. He had long been the sword for his people, but now he was the head. A duty he could no more shirk than the previous assignation.

"Eventually."

"With all due respect, Sheikh, the delay in producing an heir is what finds us both here today. I failed to have a child with my husband when I could have, and your brother failed to do so, as well. Therefore I find myself displaced. My brother-in-law is as uninterested in taking me as his bride as I am in becoming her, and you are here on the throne permanently when it should likely be a nephew of yours assuming the position. If I've learned one thing over the past year, it's that delay in procreation can be quite a costly error."

Tarek leaned back, his muscles aching. This past month in the palace had done nothing to acclimatize him to modern furnishings. He found the positions they required him to hold unnatural.

His original assessment of this queen, Olivia, was that she was fragile. He was beginning to wonder if he had been blinded by appearances. He knew better than that.

A man who had spent as many years out in the desert as he had knew better than to trust his eyes alone. Mirages were more than the stuff of legend. As he well knew.

In the desert you were far more likely to find sand than any respite from the heat. Still, when news of Malik's death had been brought to him by the leader of the Bedouin tribe he spent some of his time with, he had been reluctant to return.

What could he offer the country as a diplomat? This country that was a part of his soul. A nation left devastated by his brother's rule. By the loss of his parents all those year ago to an assassin's bullets.

This country he had sworn to protect at all costs. Because it was all that remained. The throne, the protection of Tahar, were the very reasons his parents had lost their lives.

Which was why he had to return. Why he had to rule. Why he had to continue on. Why he had to heal this nation left broken and in ruins by Malik.

And why, no matter how distasteful it might seem, he had to consider the merit of taking a bride. One who would fill in the gaps he could not.

"On that you present a well-made point. And yet, I have other options. At the very least I have proved I am much more difficult to kill than my brother."

She arched her pale brow. "Is anyone actively trying to disprove that? Because my own safety is paramount in my mind. If you have enemies, I find it won't do to put myself, or any potential children, in that sort of situation."

"I appreciate your self-interest. However, my brother's death was nothing more than an accident. There are no enemies. Any detractors he might have had he dealt with harshly. None remain."

"The manner of ruling ensures that many in fact remain. It's just they are silenced. Hopefully, you do not bear the brunt of their anger."

"I am not Malik. I do not intend to follow his example." Far from it. He intended to rule for the people, not for himself. Malik had intimidated the masses. Had ignored the economy. Had turned a blind eye while people starved. Spent money on lavish parties and bought jewels and penthouses for his latest courtesan. He had served no master but his own lust, and Tarek refused to walk down that same path.

Far better to resent power than to crave it. As Tarek now knew his brother had done from when he was a very young man. As he had learned in greater depth since he'd returned.

His brother was a murderer. Thankfully, now a dead one.

She nodded slowly. "I see. Change can cause its own issues."

"You speak as though you have experience with this."

Pale pink lips curved upward. She was such a refined

creature. Foreign to him. He had spent very little time in the company of women, less so women such as this.

The females who populated the Bedouin camps he frequented were strong, accustomed to a harsh way of life. To fending off the elements and intruders, both from nature and enemy factions. They were not like this ridiculous and impractically designed specimen before him. Willowy, slim, with a neck that was too long and fragile in his estimation. She appeared far too easily broken.

"My husband made quite a few changes when he took the throne. He was responsible for a great deal of modernization. Alansund was one of the more outdated countries in Scandinavia and King Marcus did quite a lot to change that." She swallowed, that lovely, impractical throat working. "Change is always painful."

He nodded slowly. "And your country faces another change. A new king."

"Yes. Though I trust Anton will do his best for the country. He's a good man, my brother-in-law."

"Not good enough for you to marry?"

"He is involved with someone else and wishes to marry her. Anyway, it's a bit biblical. Taking your dead brother's wife. Not to mention, it didn't settle well with me."

Tarek could not imagine why she would find that specifically objectionable. He tried to imagine what it might have been like if Malik had been in possession of a wife. He couldn't fathom why it should be more distasteful than any other method of acquiring a sheikha. It didn't matter to him who the woman had been married to previously.

But then, he had to acknowledge his ignorance when it came to relationships between men and women. Perhaps, it was one of those things that escaped him due to the singular nature of his existence prior to coming back to live in the palace.

"It was he who sent you here? Your brother-in-law?"

She nodded slowly, taking a step toward the throne, the sound of her shoes on the black marble unique to his ears. Something to do with the high-heeled style of her footwear. Intriguing. Unfamiliar.

"Yes. He realized you might be in need of a queen. And it so happened we had an extra."

He recognized the bit of strange humor in that statement. He might have laughed had he been a man given to such things. As it was, he had forgotten how.

"And we are short one. I can see where this appeared to be a logical solution. But regrettably I find I'm in no space to make vows. Now, are you able to see yourself out or shall I call some guards to assist you?"

Olivia couldn't remember the last time she had been dismissed. Or perhaps she could. In reality Anton had summarily dismissed her across the sea and to a foreign country to make herself an asset to Alansund. Because with Marcus dead she no longer qualified as important. It was pointless to be angry about it. She had no royal blood. She had borne no heir. That was palace life. None of it was personal.

The health of the country was paramount. When she had married Marcus she had pledged her allegiance to her adopted homeland, and she could hardly give it up now that he was gone.

In truth, this was the second relationship Anton had attempted to arrange for her. The first to a diplomat from Alansund who would be taking up residence in the United States. Since Olivia was American by birth it had made sense, but...

She'd felt no connection to the man. And the idea of returning to the US had felt like a regression somehow. She wanted something new. Craved it.

Then Malik had died and a new sheikh had been installed in Tahar. The perfect opportunity to forge an alliance with a country long isolated, but rich in oil and other resources.

Anton had asked, and she had agreed. She'd failed him once; she wouldn't do it again. Still, even knowing the sheikh was unconventional, raised mainly in the desert, she had imagined…something else. She certainly hadn't expected this man.

His presence filled the throne room with an animalistic air that radiated from him. He was not the sort of royalty she was accustomed to. Her husband and her brother-in-law were cultured. Men who spoke with carefully chosen words, who had posture that would cause envy in the most experienced soldier. Men who wore suits with expert precision—aristocratic beauty so sharp it was deadly.

Sheikh Tarek al-Khalij possessed none of those qualities. He was more beast than man, leaning back on the glittering throne, one hand on his chin, the other holding fast to the ornate armrest. His legs were spread wide, one outstretched, the other tucked beneath the chair.

He was not handsome.

In his unremarkable tunic and linen pants, with his long black hair pulled back by a leather strap and his dark beard concealing most of these features, he was the furthest thing from it.

But he was captivating.

His eyes were like onyx—endless, flat. Assessing. She found it difficult to look away.

In many ways she was relieved that he was turning her down. This was not what she had signed on for. She'd seen pictures of the previous ruler. He had been cultured, handsome in much the same way Marcus had been.

She had been prepared to take on another man such as that. She had not been prepared for Tarek.

Still. She had no idea what would become of her if she

turned back now. If she returned to Alansund without completing the proposed mission. If she slipped straight back into the void of grief and uselessness she'd been wallowing in at the palace. And she desperately didn't want to disappoint her brother-in-law. Didn't want to sever one of the few good ties she had in place.

She imagined that Anton wouldn't disown her completely. But there was no place for her there. No purpose. She would have nothing more to do than rattle around the large palace, nothing more than a useless limb that could easily be amputated. Until she said something. Until she spoke up and lost the good favor of the last person on earth who cared about her even a little…

It was too close to what she'd experienced growing up. The forgotten child. Because everyone had had to give Emily every last shred of attention. Watching Emily required constant vigilance. The state of her health needing to be monitored at all times.

What does resenting that make you?

She pushed the thought to the side. It didn't matter. None of it mattered. Her parents had done what good parents had to do. And she had done what a good sister should. Still, she had an aversion to idleness. To invisibility.

"I wish you would reconsider," she said, the words exiting her lips before she had a chance to think them through.

Did she wish he would reconsider? She wasn't sure. Part of her wanted to run away, to go back to the private plane that had brought her here—the same sort of plane her husband had perished in two years ago—climb into the bed and cover herself with a blanket and spend the flight back to Alansund curled into the fetal position.

That was the other problem. Returning would require getting on a plane again. Three antianxiety pills had not been enough to make that bearable.

She'd never liked to fly. Losing Marcus hadn't helped that particular phobia.

"Do you know what my function has long been here in my country?" His tone was mild. Deceptive, she had a feeling.

"Enlighten me," she said, schooling her tone into smooth unbreakable glass.

"I am the dagger. The one a man might keep hidden in the folds of his robe. Concealed, and all the more dangerous for that reason. I did not command the army. Rather, my place was in the desert. My focus on the tribes there, on ensuring stability. Loyalty to the crown. Commanding small battalions when need be. Crushing insurgency before it ever had the chance to take root. The enemy to my brother's enemies. The one they barely knew existed. They say if you live by the sword, you will also die by it. If that is the case, I suppose I am simply awaiting the final blow. However, as I previously stated, I am quite difficult to kill."

Unease crept down her spine like icy fingers. If he had been intending to scare her, he had very nearly succeeded. But he had also piqued her curiosity. And for the moment that overrode the fear.

"Do you have any training in being royalty?" she asked.

"Do I know how to converse with foreign dignitaries, give speeches and eat with rudimentary table manners? No."

"I see," she said, taking a step closer to him. She felt as if she was approaching a caged tiger. There was no real danger, not in this setting. But the strength, the lethal potential in his body was evident. "With that taken into account, perhaps I could be of use to you in other ways?"

"What other ways? If you mean to entice me with your body—" he looked her up and down as he said the word, his gaze dismissive "—you will find that I am not so easily moved."

Heat rushed over her in a flood. She wasn't sure if it was embarrassment or anger. And she wasn't sure why she would feel either. She didn't know the man. His assessment of her body didn't mean anything to her. She was confident enough in her appeal. Marcus had certainly never had any complaints.

She did her best to keep from flinching. To keep from faltering. Her emotions, her concerns, had no place here. Truly, she had no right to feel upset, or concerned. She owed this to Anton. He wasn't asking too much, not when it came to serving the country.

"Any woman can share her body with you," she said, her tone dismissive. "Very few have the benefit of royal training. As I said, I'm American. An heiress, and certainly from a wealthy family, but not royal. There was much I had to learn before I was ready to become queen. I could teach you."

His expression barely changed, a flicker in his eyes that was nearly imperceptible. "You think I might find value in that?"

"Unless you want the country you've spent so much of your life protecting to burn, I think you will. There is an entirely different manner of strength that is coveted in politics. And like your physical strength, you will be required to work at it. You must build up your muscles, so to speak."

"I don't have to marry you to receive the benefit of your training."

"It's true. You don't. And perhaps that's a good place for us to start."

"What are you proposing?"

"Give me some time to prove my value to you. Marriage is a rather serious step for two strangers to take."

He tilted his head to the side. "Have you married one before?"

"Marcus wasn't a stranger when we married. We met at university."

"A love match?" he asked, one dark brow raised.

Her stomach twisted uncomfortably, a bit of numbness starting at the tips of her fingers and slowly spreading upward. "Yes." She swallowed hard. "Just another reason I find it so easy to entertain the idea of a mutually beneficial alliance. I am not searching for, nor do I anticipate having, another marriage like my first. I don't want one."

"I can promise you a marriage between the two of us would be nothing like the one you shared with your first husband."

She didn't doubt it.

"Fine. Don't send me back. Give me one month. I will help you with the finer points, and we can engage in a kind of courtship. A bit of something for the media, something for your people. If it doesn't work out, there is no harm. But if it does... Well, it solves several problems."

He stood abruptly, his movements fluid. It reminded her of the strike of a viper. So still in the moment just before the fatal hit was administered. Over before you ever knew it had occurred.

"Dowager Queen Olivia of Alansund, we have an accord. You have thirty days to convince me that you are indispensable. If you are successful, I will make you my wife."

CHAPTER TWO

"A MEMBER OF staff will show you to a room."

"Perhaps you might trouble yourself just long enough to show me?" Olivia didn't know why she was pressing for any more time spent in Tarek's presence. Perhaps it was simply her attempt at reclaiming control of the situation.

She didn't like feeling out of control, and the past two years of her life had given rise to the feeling that she was nothing more than a rock hurtling through space, at the mercy of gravity's pull. She hated that feeling. It was too close to what she'd experienced growing up with the specter of terrible illness hanging over the household.

Nothing highlighted your true lack of influence on anything important like death, or the threat of death. Olivia was far too familiar with both.

So you can wallow in it, or you can make a difference. It isn't like Anton wants to send you on an unpleasant mission. But he has a country to consider.

And so did she.

This wasn't the time to break down. This wasn't the time to start making things all about her, and her comfort. There was a broader scope to consider.

"You assume I might know where a prepared guest room is. I assure you I do not."

"You don't know the layout of the rooms in your own palace?"

He stepped down from the raised platform the throne

sat on, making his way toward her. "This is not my palace. It is my brother's palace. That is my brother's throne. I wear my brother's crown. Metaphorically, of course." Olivia found it impossible to breathe with Tarek advancing on her as he was. He was nothing like the men she was accustomed to. Nothing like her gentle, sophisticated father. Nothing like her cultured, amusing husband. Or indeed her quiet and steady brother-in-law. If she was focusing on space metaphors, Tarek was a black hole. Sucking the air, the sound, the energy from the room around him, internalizing it. Creating a void that he alone commanded. "None of this is mine. I was not meant for this. If you intend to make me your project, then you should be aware of that fact."

"What is the solution, then? Because you seem to be here, whether or not you feel destined for it," she said, not certain where the strength to speak came from. Apparently, though he had sucked the air from her lungs, he had not stolen her ability to speak.

"I suppose you are the solution. My brother's advisers despair of me. Fair enough, as I despair of them. I feel they are weak-minded sycophants, trained to be so by a ruler who required mindless servitude. I do not. Nor do I want it."

"Come now, most rulers enjoy a bit of bowing and scraping."

Black eyes clashed with hers. "Only a man craves praise. A weapon wants nothing more than to be used. And that, my queen, is all that I am."

She swallowed hard, trying to appear self-possessed. Trying to feel self-possessed. "Then, I will train you to fight. The way a king must fight."

He began to pace, making a circle around her. A shiver ran through her, chilling her down to her bones. "I worry. I worry about the things I have left behind, untended."

"Then, use what you have seen. I'm sure you know more about many things than your brother ever did." She had no idea if that was true; she was simply trying to prove her worth. "Use that. And let me assist you with the rest. Interacting with diplomats is simply politics as usual. My husband excelled at that. As do I."

"Well, then, I expect for you to prove that within the allotted time. Follow me." He strode past her, his movements decisive, abrupt.

She snapped to attention, doing her best to keep pace with him. It was nearly impossible. The top of her head came to his shoulder, and that was with the aid of her high heels. She had to take three strides to his every one, sounding like a panicked baby deer as she clicked along the marble. "Where exactly are you taking me? Because you just said you didn't know where you were going."

"Give me a skin of water, place me in the middle of the desert and I could find my way back. And yet, I find this palace difficult to navigate. It is too dark. I depend on the sun for my direction."

"Interesting," she said, "except, are you leading me to my room or the middle of the desert? Inquiring minds want to know."

Just then a servant girl turned the corner and began walking toward them down the long corridor, her eyes averted. "You there," Tarek said, his tone commanding. "Are there guest quarters in which I might install the queen?"

The girl stopped, her eyes widening. "Sheikh Tarek, we did not know to expect a guest."

"Yes, because I did not tell you we were expecting one. Though I assumed my impotent advisors might have done. It is extremely difficult to accomplish simple tasks here. In the desert each man asks for himself. We have none of this foolish bureaucracy."

The girl looked at him, her expression blank.

"I'm fine with whatever is available," Olivia said, attempting to inject some diplomacy into the exchange. "I'm certain it will be fine. So I will need my bags brought from the car."

The girl nodded. "I can do that. The room nearest the sheikh's quarters has a made-up bed. It will be the simplest room to prepare."

Tarek went very still, and Olivia had the feeling he didn't want her staying near him. "That will be fine," Olivia said before he could protest. Her aim was to be in proximity with him after all.

"See that it is done," Tarek said.

The girl nodded and scurried off.

"I imagine you know how to find the room," Olivia said.

He nodded once. "Indeed. Follow me."

They wandered down a maze of domed corridors, with silver walls inlaid with stone reflecting off the polished floor. The palace at Alansund housed the crown jewels of the royal family. This palace seemed to be made of them. It was ostentatious, a show of riches that awed even her.

"This is beautiful."

He stopped, turning to face her. "Is it? I find it oppressive."

He turned away again, continuing to lead them in their journey. He was such a strange man. Impenetrable as rock, and yet, at the same time, honest in his speech. Still, for all that honesty, she found she could not understand him.

"I suppose when you are used to open spaces, it might be difficult to become used to living behind stone walls."

"I'm used to stone walls. I've spent much of my time inhabiting caves, and an abandoned village out in the middle of the desert. But I have no good memories here." He let his words die there, and she sensed there would be no reviving them now, no matter how persistent she was.

She didn't need him to go on. She didn't need to know his story, didn't need to understand him.

She simply needed him to marry her.

A wave of fear, of uncertainty, washed over her. She wondered what she was doing here. Why she was agreeing to marry this stranger.

For Alansund. Because you were asked to. Because you are a queen who has no throne, no power. Because you have no husband. Because you have nowhere else, and nothing else.

Her internal voice had ample reason, and she found it difficult to argue. But fear was not looking for rationality. Fear was simply looking for a foothold, and it had found one.

Not so difficult to do in this situation.

Still, she followed on. He paused at one of the ornate doors that led to what she assumed would be her quarters for the duration of her stay. He pushed the door open without saying anything.

"You're a scintillating conversationalist, has anyone ever told you that?" she asked.

"No," he said, the sarcasm skating right over his head.

"I'm not that surprised."

"Conversation was never required of me."

In that statement, she felt all of the helplessness he would never otherwise express. And somehow, in that moment, with those words, she felt a connection with him. They were both in a situation they were ill equipped to handle. Olivia, having lost her status, having lost the man that was so much a part of her identity. And Tarek, pulled from the desert to become something he had never been trained to be.

"We will find a way," she said. She wasn't sure who the assurance was really meant for. Him, or her.

"And if we do not, you can return home."

"It isn't my home," she said, speaking the words that terrified her more than any others. "I don't have one. Not now."

"I see. I have one. I simply cannot return to it."

"Perhaps we will make one here?"

She tried to imagine finding a bond with this man, tried to imagine being his wife, and she found it impossible. Though not more impossible than returning to Alansund. Watching her brother-in-law sit on the throne, where Marcus had been before. Watching his fiancée take *her* place.

That was perhaps an even bigger impossibility.

"If not that, perhaps we can simply prevent the palace from falling into ruin? And the entire country with it?"

"That's a lot of faith you're placing in a stranger," she said.

"I would more readily put my faith in you than anyone who worked under my brother."

"Was he so bad?"

"Yes," Tarek said, offering no further explanation. And she could tell, by the finality in that one-word answer, that he would not.

"Then, perhaps you don't have as far to go as you might think. You may look good simply by comparison."

"Perhaps."

Olivia didn't say anything; rather, she continued to stand next to him, feeling intensely uncomfortable. Socially at sea. That almost never happened to her.

"I thought you wanted to be shown to your room," he said.

"I do," she said, walking past him and into the vast space. Different than her quarters in Alansund, but no less grand. It glittered like the rest of the castle, full of gold and jewels, the bed wrought from precious metal, twisted together like gilt tree branches. "I suppose I just feel a bit—" She turned as she spoke the sentence, and saw that she was talking to nothing.

Tarek had excused himself without a word. Obviously finished with her for the moment.

She was alone. Something that had become far too common in recent months.

How she hated the emptiness.

She crossed the room, taking a seat on the edge of the bed, trying to squash the feeling of terror, of sadness climbing up inside her, mixing together to create a potent cocktail that made her head swim, made it difficult to breathe.

"You can't break now," she said. "You must never break."

He wasn't sure if it was a memory or a dream. Both.

Right now, though, it was agony, reality. As it had been ever since he had come back to the palace. Ghosts of the past long banished rising back up to haunt him.

He had spent a great many years out in the middle of the desert with nothing but a sword to act as protection. There, he had known no fear. Because the worst that had awaited him was death. Not so here in the palace. Here, there was torture.

He sat up, his breath burning like fire, sweat rolling down his face, his chest. He was disoriented, unsure of his positioning in the room. Certain, in that moment, that he wasn't alone.

He was on the floor, a blanket tangled around his naked body. He stood, disengaging himself from the fabric, searching the dark space around him, his every sense on high alert. He felt as if he was dying. His brain lost in a cloud of fog that made it impossible to sort through what raged inside him, and what he had to fear outside.

He walked to his nightstand and took his sheathed sword from the surface. Something wasn't right about any of this, but he couldn't sort through what it might be. There was nothing in his mind but a tangle of demons, and he couldn't see around them to figure out what his next action should be. So he defaulted to what he knew.

Violence. And the intent to draw blood before any could be shed by him.

He pulled the sword from the scabbard and held the blade high, walking toward the door, toward the threat.

A thunderous sound woke Olivia from her sleep. She sat upright, her hand pressed to her chest, her heart beating fast. Instinctively, because she was confused, disoriented, she looked to her left, checking to see if Marcus had heard the sound, too.

But of course he hadn't. Because he wasn't there.

He was dead. She knew that. Was unbearably conscious of it almost all the time. Forgetting now, in a palace in a faraway land, in the bedroom next to the man she was considering marrying in place of Marcus... It seemed cruel.

She heard the sound of metal scraping against stone and clutched the blanket more tightly. For the first time she questioned her safety. She had made a lot of assumptions about Tahar, about Tarek, based on the fact he was a royal. Based on the fact that this was a palace. Based on her position. She questioned all of it now. Now, when it was too late.

She got out of bed, grabbing hold of her robe, sliding the diaphanous fabric over her flimsy nightgown. She pushed her hair back from her face and walked quietly toward the door, the marble cold beneath her feet. That unbearable curiosity of hers was warring with her sense of self-preservation.

You are being overdramatic. You are in a palace. You're a visiting political ally. Nothing is going to happen to you.

She was just firmly in that place of paranoid thinking she'd been knocked into after Marcus's sudden death. Where everything was potentially fatal, and most certainly out to get her. She blew out a determined breath and took another step to the door, cracking it cautiously, peering out at the corridor.

Her breath froze completely in her lungs when she caught sight of the figure prowling in the darkness. A man, large, imposing. Naked. In his hand was a sword, a deadly, curved blade glinting in the moonlight that filtered through the high-set windows that lined the long hall.

She should be terrified. And she was, rivulets of fear sliding through her, freezing, increasing the icy terror that wound itself around her lungs. She was also fascinated.

He turned, long hair sweeping to the side with the movement, and she caught sight of his face. Tarek.

He didn't look like anything that should be here in this time. He was like a relic of a bygone era. A Viking warrior or fierce desert marauder. His chest was broad, thick, the muscles of his arms massive. They would have to be to wield the sword the size of the one in his hand. He was a statue made flesh, the perfect specimen of a man lovingly crafted by an artist's hands. Brought to deadly, feral life.

He turned away again, prowling down the same length of hall he had done the first time before coming back, moving toward her room. She froze, stopping her breath. She would have stopped her heart for a moment if she had the power. But just like before, he ended his march at the edge of the door to his chamber. A sentry, on guard, weapon in hand.

He didn't know where he was, that much she was certain of. Though she couldn't be entirely sure why she was certain. Perhaps simply because she was reasonably sure he wouldn't normally stand watch without anything to cover his body.

A shaft of light fell across his bare back, highlighting

the ridges of muscle along his spine and down lower. Now she couldn't breathe even if she wanted to.

Her heart thundered a hard and even beat, the blood in her veins running hotter. Faster.

She had no explanation for it.

Except that it had been two years since she'd touched a man. But surely she wasn't that basic.

So basic that she found herself captivated by a naked man holding a sword, a stranger, when she should be afraid and possibly calling for help.

But her mouth didn't work anymore, her throat too dry for words to escape.

When he turned again, the light fell across his face. In that moment, it wasn't his beauty she was captured by, but his torture. His pain. It was there, evident in the lines etched into his skin, in the deep hollowness of his eyes.

She could feel his pain. As though it had invaded her own chest, wrapping itself around her heart and squeezing tight.

That was when she closed the door. There was an ornate key jammed into the lock and she turned it, securing herself in the chamber. She wasn't sure she was locking him out, or locking herself in. She wasn't sure of much at the moment.

She grabbed the edges of the robe and held it more tightly around herself, climbing back into bed and covering her head. All she could hear now was the beating of her own heart, her own ragged breathing.

She had a feeling it would be a very long wait for sunrise.

CHAPTER THREE

TAREK FELT AS though he hadn't slept. Odd, considering he now lived in a palace, when before he had lived in the hollowed-out shells of houses not inhabited by anyone other than him for the past two hundred years. One would think he would find better rest protected by guards, in a temperature-controlled environment. With a mattress. And yet, he found he didn't.

He'd been awake for only an hour, and already he had been accosted by several members of staff while walking through the halls. So many decisions that had to be made before he had seen to his morning routine.

In the desert, he had started a fire early every morning, boiled water for coffee. Usually he ate bread or an instant hot-cereal packet he acquired from different traders that came and did business with him every few months.

He spent the morning getting into the rhythm of the day. Tasting the weather on his tongue, getting a sense for what the earth had in store for him. He worked hard, and when his brother had need of him, he did dangerous, bloody business. But he would also go many days in a row without ever speaking to another person. Without doing much beyond physical training and tending to his encampment.

When trouble was brewing, he would attach himself to the Bedouin camps, rallying with the men to see what could be done to protect their borders. Otherwise, he led a solitary existence.

The palace was never solitary. There were people moving about constantly. And it all seemed to revolve around him.

He didn't like it. Not at all. He was the man who waited. Who said, "Here I am, send me." He was the weapon. He was not the one who wielded it.

He was now in pursuit of coffee. The breakfasts they served here in the palace were too ornate for his liking. Cheese and fruit, cereals, meats. His brother had always lingered over meals. And Tarek had begun to believe that any indulgence his brother had was one that might cause corruption. Was one he ought to abstain from.

Food, in his estimation, was yet another tool designed to complete a specific task. It was simply fuel.

Coffee was a slightly more necessary fuel. A part of his routine he could not forgo.

He walked into the dining room and saw Olivia sitting at the head of the table, a bit of the type of food he had just been thinking of spread out over her plate. She looked up, smiling. She had a pleasing smile. Pink lips, even, white teeth. He liked the look of it.

He quite liked the look of her.

Much like lingering over food, he had never much lingered over women.

"Good morning," she said. A dull blush rose in her cheeks. That, he felt, was also pleasing.

"Good morning." He felt obliged to return the greeting, though he didn't agree with her assessment.

"How did you sleep?" she asked.

"I would imagine not well. I'm still tired."

She nodded slowly. "Oh. You don't have any insight about why?"

A strange flash of memory broke over him. Terror. Pain. Restlessness.

He shoved it aside. These memories, memories long

suppressed, had taken on new life when he'd returned. An even more violent life when he'd discovered his brother's private journals.

Admission that Malik had ordered the death of their parents. A secret Tarek could never share with the country, for they had suffered so much already at the hands of Malik. His spending had left people poor, bereft, taxed beyond reason with the infrastructure of the city left to decay.

He could not do further damage.

In addition to the admission of his parents' murder had been chronicles of how he'd tortured Tarek. To break him. To ensure that it was never discovered that Malik had ended the lives of the former sheikh and sheikha. To transform him into a malleable weapon to be used at Malik's discretion.

If his brother was not already dead—of an overdose, naturally—Tarek would have, in fact, killed him upon discovery of those writings.

Because Malik had never broken him. He had hardened him.

His brother had transformed him; there was no doubt. But every drop of blood Malik had spilled from Tarek's veins had soaked into the earth here. Had bound him, not to his brother, but to his nation. To his people.

He would not stray from that now.

"I do not like this place," he said.

A servant bustled into the room. "Is there anything I can get you, Sheikh Tarek?"

"Coffee. And bread."

The woman looked at him as though she feared for his sanity, but said nothing as she nodded and then left again. Only he and Olivia remained. He didn't sit; rather, he began to pace the length of the room. The hair on the back of his neck stood on end. "You know I didn't sleep," he said, turning to face her. "Tell me."

Her blue eyes widened, pale brows arching upward. "How do you know that?"

The edges of his mouth curved upward. He might have no experience of women, but he could read this one. "You become very still, very smooth when you are holding back an avalanche. There is much beneath the surface, I think. A very diplomatic woman, but occasionally you slip. You have a very sharp tongue. When you're holding it in check this well I assume it's because there is much to withhold."

The color in her face deepened, and a sense of pleasure curled itself around his stomach. Unfamiliar.

Satisfaction, he supposed.

And why not? So often he felt out of his element in this place. It was immensely rewarding to have the sense that he had claimed a victory.

To go from being the master of his domain, a man who conquered the desert, who thrived in it, to a man who could scarcely sleep. A man who was caged… It was jarring indeed. There was nothing he despised more than a sense of helplessness. And that sense of helplessness had pervaded his being from the moment he had stepped back within the palace walls. That considered, he celebrated this small victory slightly more than was necessary.

"You sleepwalk," she said, her words straightforward. Succinct. "Naked. With weapons."

Something about that word on her lips sent a burst of heat through his veins. He wasn't sure why. And yet again he was back in unfamiliar territory. Not just because of what she'd said, and how it made him feel, but because he was…doing things he didn't remember.

Out of his own control.

That settled far beyond disturbing.

"I was not aware," he said, keeping his tone flat.

"It would account for why you don't feel rested in the morning," she said. "Why don't you sit?"

"I'm not in the frame of mind to sit. I have business to attend to."

"It won't hurt you to eat breakfast," she said, a small smile playing at the edges of her mouth.

"What is so funny?"

"We already sound like a married couple." She put her hands flat on the tabletop, looking down at them. "My husband never took time for breakfast. He would eat something terribly unhealthy while he drank a coffee on his way into the office."

She looked sad, and he did not know what to do with that. "He sounds as though he was suited to this kind of life."

"He loved his country. Though he was often in a hurry in the morning because he had stayed up too late at a party the night before. And he was rushing to catch up from the moment his feet hit the ground to the moment he lay back down. He was very young, with a lot of weight on his shoulders."

"I am not so young, yet I find it quite the weight."

"How old are you?"

"Thirty. I believe."

Little lines of concern wrinkled her brow. "You aren't sure?"

"I lose track. It isn't as though anyone has ever baked me a birthday cake."

She frowned, the expression creating deep grooves by her mouth. She seemed, in his estimation, unduly distressed by his lack of baked goods. "No one?"

"Perhaps," he said, battling against a memory that was pushing against his brain. "But I would have been much younger."

It would have been when his parents were alive. And he never could remember back that far. Sometimes... sometimes he saw his father's face... So serious. So earnest. And he was speaking. But the words were muddled. He could never hear them properly.

He never tried.

Mostly because accessing those memories required him to wade through the ones that immediately preceded them. The years spent in the palace before he had been sent to the desert.

The years that had turned him to stone.

"I always had a birthday cake. Though I didn't always have anyone there to share it with me. When I was older I would go on trips with friends. Cruises and things. I made sure I didn't lack for company when I got older."

"Why didn't you always have people to share with when you were young?" He found he was interested.

"My parents were busy," she said, looking away. "I'm twenty-six. If you were curious."

"I wasn't." It was the truth. He was curious about her, but age meant little to him.

"I suppose since you aren't exceptionally curious about your own age, I can't be surprised."

"Is age something people care about?"

Her forehead wrinkled. "How long have you been out in the desert?"

"Since I was fifteen, I would say. Not solely in the desert. Primarily. I returned to the palace periodically to speak to my brother. But I rarely stayed overnight." He did not like this place. He had not liked to be in close quarters with Malik.

He had the dark thought that he liked the entire world much better now he didn't have to share it with his brother's soul.

"I'm amazed you can carry on a conversation as well as you do."

"I spent a lot of time with various Bedouin tribes. Off and on. Mostly I've lived alone. I don't dislike it."

She tilted her head to the side. "Did you dream when you were alone?"

Tarek frowned. "I don't think so."

"Did you dream last night?"

He tried to remember, but everything was fuzzy again. "It wasn't a dream. Something else. Something woke me. Pain." Memory. Not dreams. But he didn't want to tell her that.

Just then a servant appeared with a cup and an insulated pitcher, along with an assortment of rolls in a basket.

Olivia arched a brow. "Have a seat."

It hit him then, one of the things that seemed so strange about her. "You are not afraid of me." He took a seat where his food had been placed and set about pouring a cup of coffee.

"Last night I felt afraid," she said. "But you had a sword."

A sharp, hot pain lanced his chest. "I did not hurt you or threaten you, did I?"

"Would you feel bad if you had?"

He turned her question over slowly. "I have always taken the protection of women and children seriously. I would not like to hurt you. Or cause you fear."

"You speak like a man," she said, "but I wonder if you feel things like a man."

"Why?"

"You're very deliberate in your responses. Most people would know right away how something made them feel."

"I have not spent much time examining my internal workings."

She pinched her lips, her expression assessing. "You are very well-spoken. It won't be the manner in which you speak that we will find problematic, only the things you say."

"You could always write my speeches for me."

"I assume someone at the palace already does."

"I released the majority of the staff that worked under my brother."

"What did he do that made him so bad?" she asked.

Pain lanced his skull. "He just was."

"Why do you sleepwalk?"

Frustration boiled over inside him, sudden, hot. "I don't know," he said through clenched teeth. "I was not even aware that I did. How on earth would I know the reason?"

"I had to take sleeping pills for a good six months after... Sometimes sleeping is hard." She swallowed, her pale throat expanding and contracting. That part of her was pleasing, as well.

"I'm not going to take sleeping tablets. It would compromise my ability to act if the need arose."

"You're surrounded by guards here."

"You forget, I was used in addition to palace guards, and an army."

"True. But now you're the king. And I only have thirty more days."

"Twenty-nine," he said.

"No. Definitely thirty. I was only here for a few short hours yesterday, and we barely interacted."

"Twenty-nine."

She let out an exasperated breath, rolling her eyes. "You working against me will not make this pleasant."

"Sadly for you, I am not pleasant."

She stood, her hands flat against the tabletop. "And I am not pleasant when provoked. I didn't get where I am in life by being a shrinking violet." She straightened, tapping her chin with her forefinger. "The first thing you need is a haircut. And a shave. Also a suit."

"All today?"

"As I only have twenty-nine days, we may, in fact,

squeeze more into this afternoon. I don't know. It depends on how ambitious I'm feeling."

"Why does that sound ominous?"

"Because," she said, crossing her arms beneath her breasts, an action that drew his eye, "I'm also unpleasant when I'm ambitious. I have some phone calls to make. I will meet you in your office in a half hour."

With that, she turned on her heel and walked out of the room, leaving him sitting at the dining table alone.

CHAPTER FOUR

OLIVIA WAS TEMPTED to break into her antianxiety medication before meeting Tarek in his office. But no, she needed to save those for full-on panic attacks. Which, fortunately, only happened when she was boarding planes these days. She should have had one when confronted by a naked man with a sword. But panic had not been the dominant emotion.

She squared her shoulders and raised her fist to knock on his office door. She wasn't going to dwell. Not on the conflicting, heated feelings that had gone coursing through her veins when she'd seen him out in the corridor last night. Naked, tortured.

She was sick to focus on his nudity. She didn't know the man. He obviously had a great many issues. He seemed scarcely more than a feral beast.

You came prepared to marry him.

True. Which made his naked body very much pertinent to her and her interests. The idea behind marriage, after all, was for him to produce an heir.

She didn't consider sex a negative. It was part of marriage, as far as she was concerned. Not an unpleasant part. She'd never been under any illusion that this marriage agreement would mean celibacy. And in the two years since Marcus's death she had, indeed, been celibate.

She knocked, ruthlessly cutting off her line of thought. So many things were innocuous in theory and much more daunting in practice. Tarek, his body and what she felt on the subject, was one of those things.

"Enter." She heard his voice through the door.

She pushed the door open and shut it behind her, the breath rushing from her lungs at the sight of him standing in front of his desk with the posture of a soldier, hands clasped behind his back. There was no bracing for the impact of Tarek. She just needed to recognize that now and move on.

"I have entered," she said, waving a hand. "Now to get down to business."

"I am happy to take direction from you when it comes to matters of my civilization. However, that does not mean you will be assuming total control of my daily life."

"Only for the next twenty-nine days."

He chuckled, an entirely humorous sound that chilled her. "No. If you are to be my wife, then we must start as we mean to go on. I do not know how your previous marriage was conducted. However, should you become *my* wife, you must be aware of this one thing—you will not be my minder."

"I didn't think I would be," she said, her stomach tightening painfully. "And the subject of my first marriage is off-limits."

"You spoke of your husband only this morning."

She sniffed. "It's different if I broach the subject."

"Are all women so difficult?" he asked.

"Only when dealing with impossible men."

His black gaze was impassive. "Then, this should be interesting."

"That's one word for it. I assume that somewhere in the palace you have the proper tools to take care of your facial-hair situation."

"I'm not certain. We could find out." He walked over to the door of the office, swung it open and took one step

out into the corridor. And then he shouted. Possibly the
name of a servant, or just the demand, she wasn't certain.

"What are you doing?"

"I am investigating the presence of a razor. Is that not
what you wanted?"

"I assume you have a telephone on your desk. One that
might reach servants in a more direct manner than bel-
lowing like an animal."

"I did not consider that." He straightened and stepped
away from the door, closing it behind him. Then he walked
over to the desk, gazing at the phone situated there.

"Do you know how the phone works?"

"I have used it," he said, his tone clipped.

"Better idea. We go to your bathroom. I'm certain we'll
be able to find something."

"I suppose." He didn't sound convinced.

"Follow me."

She headed toward the door and felt no sense of movement behind her. She paused. "Are you coming?"

Rather than sensing any movement, she felt his heat
behind her, his breath warm on her neck. The proximity, his warmth, burned through her with the ferocity of a
spark on dry tinder. "I am not a dog to be brought to heel.
Make no mistake, my queen, I am not your pet. You are
not training me for your enjoyment. I will do what I must
to fulfill the needs of my country. But no matter the trappings I am wrapped in, the man beneath will remain the
same. I am not a good man. I'm not a bad man. I am simply a man who does what is necessary. You will do well
to remember that."

She felt the loss of his presence like a physical blow,
and she froze for a moment, gasping for breath. In that
moment, he moved ahead of her, striding out of the office
without waiting. She fortified herself, blinking rapidly, trying to gain control as she went after his retreating figure.

He blazed a path through the palace, leading them both back to the wing that contained their bedrooms. He flung open the doors to his suite wide and she followed dutifully.

I'm not a dog to be brought to heel.

Well, neither was she.

She thought her quarters were quite grand. His surpassed anything she had ever seen before. She had been a guest at many palaces during her tenure as queen of Alansund. They all paled beneath the shimmer of the palace in Tahar.

Tarek's domain could house the average dwelling. Open and vast with a massive bed at the center. The bathroom was not partitioned off from the rest of the space, a sunken tub, shower and gilt mirrors visible from where she stood in the doorway.

"I can see why you haven't found a razor. You could hide an army in here."

"Only a small army," he said. She couldn't tell if he was teasing, or being literal. It was difficult to say with Tarek.

"Small in number, or small in size?"

"Neither would be terribly helpful."

She laughed. "No, I don't suppose. Okay, if I was a razor I suppose I would hide in a cabinet. If I was a very small army, I would probably hide in a cabinet, too." She checked his face for a glimmer of humor. She saw none. "You're a tough crowd, Tarek."

"I'm not a crowd."

She shook her head and walked into the bathroom area, stopping in front of the mirror and sink, then crouching down in front of the cabinet. There was indeed a shaving kit there waiting. "Found it." She took the leather case from its position and set it on the mosaic countertop.

Tarek gripped the hem of his shirt and pulled it over his head, and all Olivia could do was stand there, her eyes wide, her lips parted. She was captivated. By his strength.

By the shift and bunch of his muscles. By the acres of golden skin covered in dark hair, and beneath that, an air of violence, of electricity that was barely contained by the flesh stretched over his bones.

He advanced on her, every inch the predator. Something in her went still, quiet.

She was, she realized, the prey. She could not run. She could not hide. And so she waited.

At the point where she saw dark spots in front of her vision she realized her subconscious had taken on a rather dramatic position. She took a sharp breath, placing herself firmly back in the moment.

"Was the strip show really necessary?" she asked.

He looked at her, one dark brow arched. "Yes. It was."

He said nothing more as he set about unzipping the bag and disseminating the contents.

There was an economy to his movements that she found fascinating. Each movement direct, capable. He was such a large man it would be tempting to think he didn't possess fine coordination. But he did. He took to readying the shaving supplies with all the skill of a man assembling a weapon.

He looked up and she studied his face as he studied his reflection in the mirror. He looked like a man regarding a stranger, not a man staring at himself.

It occurred to her then that she didn't have to stay and supervise the proceedings. But she found she couldn't tear herself away. And he didn't ask her to.

It was a terrifying feeling, being rooted to the spot like that, unable to focus on anything other than the man in front of her.

Was it so easy to attach to somebody when you had spent so much time in isolation?

Her throat ached suddenly, thinking of the empty halls of her childhood home. Of escaping that kind of solitude, finding friends, finding her place, finding her husband. And then returning to the same life. Alone. In a palace, rather than a mansion in upstate New York, but alone all the same.

Here, she had Tarek. She had a goal. A rock to cling to in a choppy sea, when before she had been adrift.

Was she so simple?

He turned the faucet on, held his hands beneath the stream of water before splashing it onto his face. Water droplets ran down his neck, down his chest. She was suddenly thirsty. *Very*, *very* thirsty.

This was just another way she was simple, apparently.

She was mesmerized by the flex in his forearms as he set about his task. He applied the same ruthless efficiency to this as he had done in the prep. The razor was a straight blade, and he wielded it with all the skill with which she had seen him wield his sword.

She had found him compelling with the beard. But the face he uncovered beneath it was simply stunning. It was a fierce kind of beauty, like the desert itself. Harsh, hard. Almost too brilliant to behold. Hard lines and unexpected curves. From his blade-straight nose to his sensual mouth. Without the competition from his facial hair, his brows were stronger, darker, framing his eyes, making them even more arresting. More powerful.

Was it only yesterday she had thought he wasn't good-looking? So much had changed between that first sighting to that unguarded moment when she'd seen him, stripped bare in every way, outside his chamber. To this moment here, as he scraped away another layer, revealed yet another facet of himself.

When he finished, he pooled water into his hands again, rinsing away the remaining soap and the odd stray whisker still clinging to his skin. He straightened and turned to look at her, and it was almost as if she was seeing a different man.

Except for those eyes. Those eyes were undeniable.

His dark hair was wet, hanging loose down to his shoulders. He would have to get that dealt with as well, but she didn't expect him to do that on his own. She almost thought it was a shame. There was something arresting about him as he was now, something disreputable about the long hair. A nod to the fact that he appeared to be, in many ways, a relic of the past.

She took a step toward him, and he stayed, immovable as stone.

Her heart was thundering so hard that if he spoke, she wouldn't be able to hear him over the sound echoing in her ears. She felt compelled to close the distance between them. She knew one moment of hesitation, one moment where she thought she might be better off showing restraint. But why? There was no reason to show restraint of any kind. No reason to suppress the buzz of attraction she couldn't deny she felt for him.

Maybe she felt it only because it had been so long since she'd been with a man. Maybe she felt it only because she was lonely. But maybe, just maybe, the reasons didn't matter. Her ultimate goal was to marry him after all.

Chemistry was a very powerful reason for marriage, as far as she was concerned.

There would be no harm in testing that chemistry.

She looked at him, tried to assess what he was thinking. Searched for knowledge deep in his eyes about what would come next. She saw nothing. Nothing but an abyss. And yet, like a child drawn to a bottomless well, she kept on moving toward him.

He smelled like clean skin and the soap he had just used, and there was something about the simplicity, the intimacy of that, she found irresistible.

Somewhere in the back of her mind a logical voice was telling her to think through her actions. Was tapping her shoulder and reminding her that, though she had come here with the aim of marrying him, Tarek was a stranger. That she had waited two months to give Marcus so much as one kiss, and waited until she had been given an engagement ring before she shared her body with him.

That she was dangerously close to exposing parts of herself she should hide for her protection. Because she knew what happened when she stepped out of bounds. When she made waves.

She ignored that voice, because while it spoke the truth, it was telling the truth about the girl she had been. Not the woman she had become.

Tarek was a man. Not a boy barely out of university. And she would appeal to him as a woman appealed to a man.

She reached up, brushing her fingertips over his cheekbone, down along the line of his jaw. His skin was smooth now, the sensation intoxicating. She felt him tense beneath her touch, a muscle in his cheek jerking. "It's very nice," she said, drawing closer still.

Her heart was thundering hard, her breasts aching, her nipples tight and sensitive. She lifted her other hand, pressing her palm flat against his chest. He was so hot. So hard. She moved her hand slightly, intent on trailing her fingertips down his abs, but she found herself wrenched away from him, stumbling backward.

Those black eyes were fearsome now, his chest, the chest she had just barely touched, heaving with the force of his breath.

"What are you doing, woman?"

And suddenly the thoughts that had been nothing more than a niggle in the back of her mind blanketed her completely, suffocating her. What was she doing? He had given no indication he wanted this. She barely knew the man.

Belatedly, she snatched her hand back against her chest, holding it in tightly. As though contracting in on herself now would make him forget she had ever reached out to him.

Then she wondered why, why she was allowing herself to feel embarrassed. Why she should bother to cover up the impulse. If they were to be married, they would have to come to an agreement on this. She wasn't going to spend the rest of her life pretending to be a different woman. Pretending to want different things than she did. Truthfully, she was a bit shocked she wanted much of anything with him, considering he was a stranger. But she did. And in many ways, it was fortuitous. Being married to a man she wasn't attracted to would be a hideous fate.

"I was touching you," she said, her tone hard. "Is that so shocking?"

"For what purpose?"

She stared at him, hard, trying to work out if he was being disingenuous. "Because I wanted to touch you."

"Don't."

"If we marry, that could be a problem."

"If we marry, we can deal with it then."

"Oh, I don't think so. It's important that we deal with these sorts of things now." She swallowed hard. "I expect for this to be a real marriage."

"It could hardly be a fake marriage." He turned away from her, stalking back to the center of the room, bending over to pick up his shirt. "It will have to be legal, obviously."

"Paperwork isn't all there is to it. You have to interact with the person you marry. You have to coexist together. Sexual chemistry and compatibility are important."

"If it is important to you, then, should I decide that marriage between the two of us is the most advantageous option, I will ensure your needs are met."

His words were so dispassionate, so disconnected she couldn't think of how to respond. This was not the language of seduction as she knew it. This was a one-sided conversation. He spoke as though it didn't matter to him. In her experience, sex mattered a great deal to men. And also, in her experience, having a similar appetite to one's husband was extremely advantageous.

"It is important to me," she pressed, mainly because she was so fascinated by his response. Or rather, his lack of response.

"Then, should we decide on marriage, we will deal with it."

He shrugged his shirt on and she stood there, blinking. "I don't… I'm not certain I understand."

"There is nothing to understand."

Maybe not for him, but she was confused. Never in her life had a man reacted so neutrally to her touch. Not that she was incredibly experienced. Marcus had been her only lover after all. But she had practiced flirting plenty when she'd been at school, and it had usually gone well. Her first forays into looking for attention from those other than her parents had gone well enough. It had never gone beyond very innocent kissing, but even that had been balm for her parched soul.

This was… It was far too close to that horrible, dead feeling of standing there, begging for more and receiving nothing.

Too close to that moment she'd finally told her parents she needed more than walking past each other on occasion in the halls, more than false conversation over a monthly dinner.

She was not going to think of that now.

"I imagined you would have an opinion on the topic. Men usually do."

"Men, as a species, are weak. They are fallible creatures

who have far too many appetites that demand constant satisfaction. A servant cannot have more than one master. I have learned to live for the service of my country. That means I cannot serve my own appetites, as well. Doing so would make me a weak servant indeed. The fact that I am now sheikh changes nothing. I can desire nothing greater than the desire to serve."

His words made something inside her curl in on itself. Something she hadn't realized had been trying to bloom.

What was wrong with her? Why did this matter so much?

Why did it feel so desperately personal to be rejected by a stranger?

Stop being so needy.

"I should arrange for your haircut now." It was automatic for her to get on with the task at hand. Anything was better than lingering in her discomfort and unexpected pain. "And clothing. You need to address your clothing situation."

"There is something wrong with my clothing?"

"What did your brother wear to various events? Did he wear traditional Tahari clothing, or did he wear Western-style suits? This is important. I need to figure out how to handle your wardrobe."

"I can see that if I offer you one sweet you will clamor for the whole bag."

She smiled widely, trying not to reveal the fact that the potential double entendre in his statement had hit her in a vulnerable place. Yes, it would seem that if all of this was a sexual metaphor, if he gave her one little treat, she would try to devour the whole thing. She cringed internally.

Rejection stung. Always.

"That is what I'm here for," she said, rather than giving in to saying any of the insecure things that were rolling around in her head.

"It doesn't matter to me what my brother wore. I would prefer to draw a distinction between him and myself."

"That's a good place to start," she said, not asking the questions that arose due to that statement. "What sort of ruler do you want to be? That's a question only you can answer, Tarek. Though the answer is probably also relevant to me."

"I do not believe a man is king for his own enjoyment. I believe a man can only serve if he is serving a purpose. A purpose that is beyond himself."

"You speak about serving so often."

"Bearing the responsibility of a nation is nothing if not service. If your primary objective is simply to rule, to lord over, then you accomplish nothing."

She studied him, the harsh, hard lines of his face. "If you disagreed with your brother's style of leadership, why didn't you say anything to him?"

"It was not my task. My task was very specific. And an agreement was struck between Malik and myself some years ago."

"What was that?"

"If he would leave me alone, I would be at his disposal to protect our people," Tarek said, his words layered with darkness. "A mutual agreement we both respected. He called upon me when aid was needed, and I gave it. Anything else would have been abandonment of my post, of the people I cared for. I am in a different position now."

"You have the power now. That's the brilliant thing about being sheikh. What do you want to wear? Who do you want to be?"

"I do not have the capacity to care about such a thing as clothing," he said, "but perhaps there is a connection I am missing?"

She straightened, indicating the well-fitted white dress she was wearing. "Clothing is important. It presents a certain image. I would like to think mine conveys quiet luxury and sophistication. Something people prize in a queen, or so I was told."

"I...I see how that could be."

"Good," she said. "You care about your people. I know you do."

"More than my own life," he said.

Her stomach tightened, that conviction, that bone-deep certainty of his opening up a cavern of longing from deep within. To have someone care about her with that ferocity. With that strength.

She swallowed hard. No. Even letting herself think about that was dangerous.

"We are in a new age in Tahar," he said, his tone grave. "And I am able to lead us there. I will. Let us show them."

"Well, seeing as we can't put you on the back of a white stallion brandishing a sword, I'm going to go with a power suit. I'll make some phone calls. We will be in touch."

With that, she walked out of the bathroom, out of the bedroom, and beat a hasty retreat back to her own quarters. She needed some time alone. Needed some time to think. She had to get a handle on herself, because she couldn't act in such a stupid, unthinking way again.

If nothing else, her own response to him, the emotional fallout of it, was reason enough.

She knew better than to need. Knew better than to depend on anyone.

She simply needed to remember.

CHAPTER FIVE

TAREK HAD SUCCESSFULLY avoided being directly involved in Olivia's machinations for four days. Since coming to the palace, he had craved silence with a severity that bordered on madness. Since Olivia had arrived nearly a week ago it had intensified.

Since the moment she had touched him in his bathroom it had become even worse.

He was not innocent of the ways of the world, not a fool, either. He understood what the heat and fire in his blood meant, understood why she had been touching him. But he had made vows. To the earth, to himself. He was a man of singular purpose, and that had meant eschewing earthly pleasures. When it came to food he ate to survive, and when it came to sex…

It turned out a man did not need it to survive.

In fact, he had survived thirty years without. As a teenage boy banished to the desert, he had been far too broken to care. As a man grappling with his purpose, with the memories that still crowded in at night, echoes of pain that would push any human to the brink of sanity, he had reminded himself what had brought him through. The only way to withstand torture was to focus on what lay beyond it. The bright spot. The hope. The purpose.

He had stripped back his needs to one thing so long ago that he could not remember a day when his desires had been layered. When he had relished the feel of a soft bed, enjoyed the flavor of a meal or fantasized about what it would be like to touch the lush curves of a woman's body. Memories lost to him, desires destroyed.

Every single one of them had flooded back to him the moment Olivia had placed her soft fingertips on his bare chest.

For the first time in years he had craved something sweet to eat, a sumptuous, well-appointed bed. And to see what was beneath her clothes.

That was why he had pushed her away. Contained in that one simple touch had been a weakness so complete, so repellent, he had no choice but to turn away from it.

Though she spoke the truth. Were they to be married, there would be no turning away from his duty as a husband. His duty as a sheikh.

He needed an heir.

Still, all would be possible. It was simply a matter of refocusing his purpose. And he was in the process of doing just that. They had spoken about his intentions as a ruler the other day, and as much as he would like to do nothing more than resent her presence, he had to acknowledge that she was helping. He scarcely recognized the man he saw in the mirror now. Far from the beast he had been when he had first arrived here, he now resembled someone he could imagine sitting on the throne.

His hair had been cut short. He was still getting used to the feel of it.

He felt like a man who had been pulled up out of the pit. Still orienting to the sunlight. To being aboveground.

Of course, his ability to avoid Olivia and continue to regain his equilibrium would end today. She had arranged for him to be dressed. As though he was a doll. She had been insistent that clothing was important, and when she had applied it to herself, he could well see her point.

She wore thin dresses made of luxurious fabrics that

settled over her sleek, fascinating curves in an easy manner. It was difficult to look away from her, in part because of the cut of her clothing, he was convinced. She did indeed convey authority, a sense of belonging. She could have materialized from the gems and gold in the walls of the palace, precious metals come to life.

In that way, she would make a wonderful sheikha. At least one of them would look as though they had been born to serve in a palace.

For his part, he would protect his people. That much he knew.

The doors to his bedchamber burst open wide and in came the object of his thoughts, followed by another woman he had never seen before. That woman was pushing a rack full of clothing, her expression of determination mirrored by Olivia.

"This is Serena. She is now the official dresser here in the palace. You will make use of her. Starting now."

"Hello, Olivia. It has been a few days since we've spoken," he said.

"Hi," she said. "I assume that screen over there will do for you to dress behind."

He looked between the two women, processing the idea that he would need to change behind a screen. He had no modesty to protect. He imagined, therefore, that it was for their own comfort.

He thought back to the other day. To Olivia placing her hand on his chest.

Perhaps the screen would be wise.

Serena moved the rack to the ornate divider and Tarek followed suit. He stepped behind it, grabbing the first bundle of clothing from the rack and set about undressing, and redressing. He could hear Olivia and Serena speaking in hushed tones. He had no real desire to know what it was they were discussing.

He paid no attention to what he was putting on. He had no way of assessing suitability. He simply had to trust Olivia's senses.

Serena approached him, the measuring tape in her hands, a determined expression on her face. She placed her hands on his shoulder, stretching the tape across them. And he waited. Waited for a feeling similar to the one he'd had when Olivia had touched him. But it didn't come.

There was no heat. Nothing but the cool pressure of the tape and her touch buffeted by the layers of clothing.

Olivia moved nearer to him, her hand on her chin, her expression assessing.

"Do you have a comment, my queen?"

"This works for you. Though it definitely needs to be fitted."

"I suppose it's the kind of thing I should wear to the coronation party?"

Her blue eyes flew wide. "You have a coronation party?"

"Yes."

"How is it that you haven't mentioned this before?"

"We have only had two conversations. Possibly three. One of which ended poorly." Serena knelt down in front of him, drawing the length of the tape down the inside of his leg. Olivia looked down, then back up at him, her pale brow arched. She said nothing. "Did you have something to say, Olivia?"

"Are you comfortable?"

"Do you really care?"

She pursed her lips, looking as though she was chewing her words thoroughly. "Of course I care. As your prospective fiancée. But then, as your prospective fiancée I also might have wanted to know about a major public event. There is media to consider, Tarek. We must decide whether or not we should appear together as a couple. I, for one, vote that we should."

"We have not decided what to do about our union, or lack of one."

"You have not decided," she said, her voice determined. "My decision is made. This is…where I need to be."

"Is this all about power for you?" His chest tightened, rage bleeding through him like a hemorrhaging wound. "Power corrupts, my queen. The need to rule simply for the sake of it destroyed my country once, and I will not allow that to happen again."

"That isn't what I mean. You told me once that you were a weapon. I am a queen. It chafes when you are not used as you ought to be."

"Perhaps you could fill your time as head of some sort of committee."

"That isn't what I want."

"Do you have some sort of emotional attachment to Tahar? To its success?"

She fixed determined, blue eyes on him. "I could create it."

"I don't think that's good enough, Olivia."

She took in a sharp breath, her eyes glistening. "I want a…" She looked away, then back up at him. "A home, Tarek. More than anything, I want a home that I belong in. One that isn't empty. One where I am not extraneous. You need me here. And I want to be needed. Allow me to use my skill. Allow me to be what I can be." Serena was still going about her work calmly while Olivia stood there, breathing hard, her breasts rising and falling on each indrawn breath.

"The only way to be what you want is through marriage, Olivia?" He studied her closely as he spoke. "What a frustration that must be for you. You have so little control. Or at least, this requires you to share it. Your future is dependent on my decision."

He could see Olivia's pulse fluttering at the base of her

neck. Like a panicked bird trapped in a cage. He had the overwhelming urge to place his thumb over the top of it. To feel the intensity with which it beat, the velvet softness of her skin.

That simple, brief fantasy did much more to heat his blood than anything Serena was doing with the tape measure.

"Do I have to try on everything, or will your measurements suffice?" he asked Serena.

"There is plenty I can do with the measurements," she said.

"Then, that will be all. Leave us. Olivia and I have much to discuss."

Serena scrambled to obey his command. He was accustomed to such things. To people obeying his word. He functioned in life-or-death situations. And he was the one that the tribes looked to for safety. The one his men watched to ensure that this mission was not their last.

In this, at least, he was comfortable.

"I can fetch the suit later," Serena said. She grabbed hold of the rack and made a hasty exit.

Once the door closed behind her, he and Olivia were alone. Facing each other.

He began to undo the top buttons of the shirt, and he watched as her eyes followed the motion. He was fascinated by this. By the fact that the effects he was experiencing were so closely linked to Olivia, rather than just the female form. Serena had been lovely. Dark haired, with more dramatic curves than Olivia possessed. Though he was not entirely certain if that was more enticing to him. He had given it little thought. Still, it was not outside the realm of possibility that Serena's touch *could* have set his blood on fire in the same manner that Olivia's had.

"From where I'm standing, my sheikh," she said, her tone icy, "your future, and whether or not you are able to reestablish your nation, is closely linked to me. There was no one else here helping you. Who do you have on your side? Your brother's old advisers? Those you have recently employed who are new to this position? They were going to let you attend a coronation looking as you did when I first arrived. Your people would have thought you insane. Would have thought you were a man who didn't know how to dress. One who could not be bothered to shave and represent himself as the face of the nation without looking like an overgrown bush. Have they coached you on how to deal with the press?"

For the first time, Tarek felt a bit of discomfort. For the first time, he felt lost at sea in a different way. He had been focused on acclimating to palace life. To his new position. But he had a plan. He knew what he wanted for his country, and he was confident that he was morally everything Tahar needed in a leader. But the press, a ballroom full of people… He did not know what he would do under those circumstances. He did not know how to carry on a conversation in a civil manner, much less conduct an interview, much less give speeches. He knew how to strike terror into the hearts of his enemies. Could carve a swath of death and destruction through an opposing army with a flick of his sword.

But these things? They were foreign to him.

As foreign as the heat he felt when Olivia's fingertips brushed against his skin.

He was a man who held command of life and death. A man who had survived bloody battles and great torture.

But he was, in many ways, not a man. He was all that he had been created to be. But he had not been created for this.

He would have to be remade. Again.

Sheikh Tarek al-Khalij had survived immense pain. Had faced down situations that would bring certain death, and triumphed. Very few things frightened him. But the prospect of being melted down again, reformed, did. Ice replaced the blood in his veins, a sick sensation washing over him.

He looked at Olivia, her slender form, her delicate hands. Hands that had already touched his skin. Before Olivia, how long had it been since anyone had touched him? He had had wounds bandaged at the various Bedouin camps. And before that…before that every touch had been agony. Designed to destroy.

But he could not remember the last time anyone had ever touched him so gently.

Perhaps being reformed in Olivia's hands would be a different experience.

And perhaps she was correct. Perhaps she was all the hope he had.

She had been honest with him. Pain had radiated from her blue eyes as she had spoken of having no place. She needed him. Maybe admitting he needed her would not be so terrible.

"The coronation is in two weeks," he said. "I do not know what will be expected of me."

"You set the precedent. You are the sheikh. But you have to understand that if you forgo certain things, it will appear odd."

"Did you aid your first husband in navigating his coronation?"

"I didn't have to help Marcus with any of that," she said, a soft smile on her lips. She softened when she thought of him. "He was born to that life. Created for it. He was an aristocrat on every layer. In a suit, out of the suit, you would never mistake him for anything but what he was. You, on the other hand, will have trouble looking like aristocracy even with the finest suit. I am not being insulting. I am merely stating a fact. No, I didn't help him. But I did watch him. He, in fact, helped me. I was an heiress from the States, and while I knew plenty about presenting myself at functions, royal functions are entirely different. I've walked this road. I daresay it will be longer and harder for you, but I can help you along the way."

"We shall marry," he said, his voice rough. "I know nothing about this life I have stepped into. I know what I want. I know who I want to be. But I cannot get there without you. On this you have convinced me."

Her breath left her body in a rush. "After four days?"

"You are determined. And you are very convincing." He pushed the shirt from his shoulders, standing before her in nothing more than the dress pants. "We will announce our engagement at the coronation. I feel it is best to present a strong direction for the country. That said, having a wife in waiting will be best. I'm certain you can find a wedding gown that pleases you quickly enough?"

"I can," she said, her voice soft.

For the first time since he had met her, Olivia Bretton seemed subdued. She had gone toe-to-toe with him on everything, but now that she was getting her way, she seemed to have shrunk.

"Do not wilt on me now," he said. She raised her eyes to meet his, a question flitting through them. "When I first met you, I thought the desert would cause you to wither quickly enough. But you proved to me that first day that you were made of steel. Do not disappoint me now. Not when I have admitted to needing you."

She straightened, some of the haughty defiance returning to her gaze. "I do not wilt."

"Excellent. Wilting would be no use to either of us at this point."

"You are aware that when we walk into that coronation we must look as though we are already a couple. You must be beyond reproach. You must instill absolute confidence in the stability of us as a couple. If you are looking to make us a figurehead, then we must be an infallible one. I have a reputation to stand on. The citizens of my country love me. The union will strengthen trade between Alansund and Tahar. It will be good for the economy, and will provide you with the semblance of experience."

"That will entail you hanging on my arm, I suppose?"

"I think we can forgo dancing. I highly doubt anyone would fault you. But yes, we will need to look as though we are unified in every way. You will need a speech that outlines your plans for Tahar."

"I do not have a speechwriter anymore. I fired him."

"Do you...do you write?" she asked, her voice tentative.

"I do. Though it is not a skill I often use, I admit."

"Perhaps we can work on this together. If you can lay out your plan, I can help make sure it reads well. You are well-spoken, I will say that for you."

"Something to do with spending a lot of time alone, I think."

"Why do you think that?"

"Because," he said, "I spent a lot of time speaking to myself. Keeping language was important to me, every language I learned from my father. I was quite careful with the gift he gave me." He had often spoken into the emptiness. Run through the words that he might not use with frequency. Anything to make sure he didn't lose the pieces of humanity that were still embedded in his soul. Like shards of glass, they were often uncomfortable, making them tempting to extract because they were at odds with why he had been out there in the desert. But still, he had clung to them. He was glad now.

Because now he needed it.

Too bad scattered shards were good for little when you were expected to present something unified.

"Good foresight anyway. It will come in handy later."

"I live to be handy in your estimation, my queen."

"Somehow I doubt that," she said, smiling. It was a different smile than the one that crossed her lips when she spoke of her late husband. She was a nuanced creature. And he had never been good with nuance. Weapons of destruction weren't known for nuance.

Her gaze flickered downward, and he could feel her slow perusal of his body. Then she looked back up, her cheeks red, her eyes locked with his. "You are studying me," he said.

"I find you fascinating," she replied.

"What is it about me you find fascinating?" His voice had changed, gotten huskier, deeper. And the heat was back. Heat and fire, and the dark pit of need that he had wished might remain covered.

"Right now? I find your body fascinating."

She said the words in a measured, deliberate fashion. The color in her cheeks heightened, and at the same time the fire in his veins roared ever hotter.

"I know we tabled this discussion, with marriage as the condition upon which we might speak of it again," she continued, "but now you have agreed." She took another step toward him, her hand outstretched. There was a vulnerability in her eyes he could not guess at, but appealed to some unknown, dark part of him that was previously unexplored. Temptation grabbed him by the throat, unfamiliar. And before he could fully process the decision, his body had acted.

That was not unusual. When adrenaline poured through his veins, he trusted his body to do the thinking. It was trained, finely honed, strong.

But this wasn't a battle. His body didn't care.

He wrapped his fingers around her slender wrist and tugged her forward, placing her hand flat on his chest, just over his raging heart.

An answering heat flared in her eyes and he released his hold on her, setting her free to do what she wished.

This time, when she began to forge a trail down the center of his chest to his abdominal muscles, he didn't do anything to stop her. He could not fathom how something so soft could have such a great impact. Like watching a feather land on a mountain, causing it to crumble.

Something tightened like a fist of fire in his gut, building and spreading lower, creating an ache down deep inside of him. He was the master of his body. The keeper of everything he felt, and everything he chose not to. But right now, that control had been wrenched from him. Was being clutched in Olivia's delicate grasp, those soft, velvet fingertips holding sway over his every breath, his every act. She was, in this moment, the goddess of his universe, manipulating the very air around him.

She took a step toward him, raising her other hand, curling her fingers around the back of his neck. He had seen young soldiers do the very thing he was doing now. Standing there, watching an enemy advance, knowing that fleeing was the best option but holding their ground anyway. The morbid fascination of approaching doom too great to turn away from.

For those young, untrained soldiers, facing death was an anomaly. Facing death was far too common an occurrence in Tarek's world. It held no curiosity for him in the least. But in this moment, he was much like those green young men facing down a steel-tipped arrow for the first time. Resistance should be the very first response, and yet it never was.

So he stayed, rooted to the spot, transfixed.

Though instead of watching a steel blade draw ever closer, his gaze was locked upon the clear blue of her eyes. Determined. Focused.

She paused, the tip of her tongue darting out to wet her lush, pink lips. He had the sudden image of pulling her close and completing the task for her. The urge to do so was strong, so strong his entire body shook with the restraint of not completing the task outlined in his mind's eye.

On the heels of this desire was the incongruous thought that Olivia proved an iron fist was unnecessary to wield power. A delicate touch could accomplish so much more. With it she had reached inside him, exposed cracks in the walls he'd built around himself. Reinvigorated layers of need he had spent years pretending didn't exist. Hunger became more than a simple need for fuel. It became a craving for flavor, for texture. For food, warmth, softness. For touch, and connection, and for a woman's body beneath his.

He felt split in two, at war with the desire to seize back his control and pull away from her and to follow the new, darker urges building deep inside him.

Control. Focus. Purpose. That he had to have above all else.

And this, this physical connection with Olivia, was not something he could deny. It would be part of their marriage. But he must learn to take command of it.

For that very reason he stood, allowing her to continue to touch him. He closed his eyes, forcing himself to endure. To remain passive with her hands against his skin, her fingers tangling with his hair, the other hand exploring the ridges of his muscles.

He imagined all of the heat in his blood pooling in his stomach, draining away from the other parts of him.

There he would keep it contained. There he would keep it controlled.

He drew in a ragged breath of his own accord, not commanded by Olivia, or his reaction to her.

And only then did he step away.

"What's wrong?" she asked.

"It is a very good thing, I feel, that you are fascinated with me. For it seems to be important to you. Still, I think consummation will wait until after our wedding." He felt nothing when he said the words, because he did not allow himself to think of what they meant.

"That's a very old-fashioned view."

"Values have nothing to do with this. It is about focus. I do not intend to split that focus. Mine or yours."

"I hardly think I'll have a difficult time seeing to daily tasks simply because we're in a physical relationship. You're a handsome man, but I'm not sure I'd find you quite that distracting," she said. "Though I see there is no harm in the two of us getting to know each other better. Sleeping with a stranger has never been my thing."

He looked at the feminine creature he had agreed to marry and realized that there was a very great divide between the two of them. He had seen things, terrible things. The harsh and horrible realities of life that no one should ever have to face. He had endured unimaginable, unspeakable pain that would have destroyed most men. And yet, he knew nothing of people. Nothing of relationships and connections. Nothing of heat. Nothing of passion.

She contained those secrets beneath all of that soft skin. Mysteries wrapped in mysteries that were unknown to him. They sparkled in her eyes, and he had a feeling she would share them if he but asked.

And yet, when he made the decision to add such things to his life, it truly had to be his decision. Something he controlled. Something he was certain wouldn't take away from his aims. He did not allow his body to be ruled by need. Not need for anything. Not even for the need to be relieved of pain.

And certainly not by the need for physical satisfaction.

Coming to grips with that had been more difficult when he was a boy. But he was a man with years of practice at denying unnecessary appetites. And he would continue to do so until he was certain he was in absolute control.

"I do not know if there will be a time when you won't consider me a stranger," he said, "but there will be a time when you will call me husband."

"Then, I suppose whichever comes first, you being known to me or you being married to me, will be the benchmark for when we begin a sexual relationship."

"I suppose."

She blinked rapidly, taking a sharp breath before straightening. As though she had been off balance, and had righted herself. "You are not what I expected."

"What did you expect?"

"A man," she said simply.

"In what regard?"

"I have never known a man to be so resistant to being touched. I should have thought you would consider being with me a perk of our union. Perhaps I was a bit too egotistical?"

He sensed a strain of vulnerability beneath her words, and he couldn't fathom why. She was, he gathered, hurt in some capacity by what she felt was indifference on his part.

He was not indifferent. But he felt the need to become so.

"I apologize, my queen," he said. "I have spent too many years away from people to know how one *usually* responds to anything."

She regarded him closely. "Somehow we'll make that

work to your advantage, Tarek. I'm not entirely certain how we'll make it work to *ours*."

She gave him one last look, lingering boldly over his body, then turned and walked out of his room. Leaving him half-dressed in clothes that made him feel like another man.

Or perhaps it was Olivia who made him feel that way.

CHAPTER SIX

OLIVIA WAS RESOLUTE in her decision to stay away from Tarek when he was shirtless. Because every time he stripped down, he seemed to cast her common sense to the floor right along with his clothes. She was at war with herself. Somewhat horrified by her actions while at the same time feeling completely justified in them. If he was going to be her husband, they would have to come to an agreement on this. But she would feel more comfortable if she wasn't half as invested in the agreement. If she didn't feel quite so out of control of her actions when he was near.

If she didn't want him quite so much. That was the part that horrified her. Not because she was ashamed of wanting him, but because it was exposing to desire someone like that. And to show them that you did.

She knew better than that. You played games to protect yourself. Acted a little bit coy to make sure that the man felt the same. Even when she and Marcus had been married she'd played those games. But he had, too.

She had loved her husband very much, but they had their own lives. Their own bedrooms. There were things about him she didn't know, things she didn't want to know.

She kept herself guarded. Which was just good sense.

Because she knew the alternative far too well.

Still, for some reason, keeping guarded with Tarek was difficult.

Which confounded her, since she had loved Marcus.

Known him. In that way you could know people. She had none of those things with Tarek. She had a fascination for his body. So different from her husband's. Which was a thought that made her deeply uncomfortable.

She supposed, had she had a list of lovers, the temptation to compare wouldn't be present. But as she had been with only one man, the sight and feel of another man's body was more exceptional than it might have been otherwise.

And today was speechwriting day. She was torn between the desire to spend time with Tarek, to try to understand the man she had agreed to marry, and the desire to avoid him to stop herself from making any other stupid moves.

Today, there would be no avoiding. Today, there was a speech to consider.

She smoothed the front of her plum-colored sheath dress, then patted her blond hair, neatly secured in a bun.. She looked much more collected and calm than she actually was. She had ensured that was the case before she left her quarters. She took a fortifying breath, pushing open the doors to Tarek's office. He was expecting her. She didn't see the point in knocking.

When she saw him standing there in front of his desk, his head bent low, his expression one of intense concentration, she wished that she could go back and allow herself a few more moments to fortify herself. To prepare herself.

His suit, apparently, was ready. And he was wearing it. Fitted perfectly to his broad shoulders, narrow waist, muscular thighs.

She had been right—there was no amount of expert tailoring or expensive fabric that could make him look the part of royalty. He did not look like an aristocrat. He looked like a man who had risen straight from the desert. And yet, something about the attempted civility made him appear all the more dangerous. Highlighted the ruthless lines of his face, accentuated the fearsome strength in his muscles.

"You look like you're ready to tear out someone's throat," she said, attempting to diffuse the tension that was rioting through her. A tension he was likely oblivious to.

"Always," he said. "I do what I must."

"Terrifying, Tarek. Very terrifying." She was being dry, and yet she sensed his words were true.

The thought sent a shiver through her body, and she couldn't work out whether it was one of fear, or one of arousal. There was a thin line separating the two when it came to Tarek. She found it unnerving.

"Unless you mean to harm my country in some way, you have nothing to fear from me."

Somehow she very much doubted that. Somehow she felt that she might have quite a bit to fear from him. She wasn't sure where that came from, why she knew it all the way down to her blood. Only that she did.

She shook off the foreboding sensation. "Then, we should be fine."

"I am uncertain about the speech."

"I am here to help you be certain."

That statement resulted in her having a stack of papers thrust in her direction. The words on the page were handwritten, and it was obvious that wielding a pen was not as familiar to him as wielding a sword.

"You couldn't have typed this?" she asked. She supposed that was a ridiculous question. The man had not thought to use the phone sitting on his desk to reach members of staff.

"No."

"I'm sorry. Do you know how to use a computer?"

"I haven't done so in a great many years."

"Well, the thing about technology is that it changes. It's likely you will have to learn to do it all over again." She perused the papers in her hand. "But that isn't important right now. This is important. One thing at a time."

The speech wasn't eloquent. She couldn't lie. There was no point.

"Okay. I think this is a decent guideline for what you might want to say. It is your heart. It's what you want to do for the country. And I have spoken to you, and you speak well. So." She handed the papers back to him. "You can use this if you get lost. But I want you to just tell me what you want for Tahar. What your plans are for the future. Make it brief, because people have limited attention. And you don't want to overpromise. Better to overdeliver."

"I don't know how to speak in front of people."

"I bet that isn't true. You…" She searched for the right words. "You commanded men. You had to rally them before you went into battle. Didn't you?"

"Yes."

"This is the same thing. It's a rally cry. For your people. Things might look bad now. They might seem hard. But nothing is impossible. You have faced down enemies and triumphed. You will triumph now. And so will they."

He arched a brow. "I feel that perhaps you should give the speech for me."

"Too bad it's never the spouse they want to hear from. Unless it's a garden party. Perhaps the opening of the children's hospital."

"More things I must manage, I take it."

"No," she said, tempted to touch him. Knowing she shouldn't. "I'll be your softer side. You sound the battle cry."

"That sounds doable. Oftentimes none of this does."

"That's marriage. I'm your other half. No, we don't love each other. But I don't think we have to in order to fulfill that. I have skills you don't. And you carry this country in your blood. You're a warrior. So many things I could never be. But together we will make this work."

Just saying the words made her feel as if things were locking into place inside her. Gave her a sense of completeness, of rightness. Being a part of something instead of sitting alone in the dark.

He looked up, his dark eyes meeting hers. "I need you to be more than half right now," he said. "Because I feel I have little to contribute."

"That's okay," she said, swallowing hard, the lingering emotion from her earlier realization making her ache. "Sometimes you might have to be more than half for me."

"Should that ever arise, I swear that I will."

It wasn't passionate. It wasn't romantic. It was nothing like the declaration of love she and Marcus had shared over a dinner on his family yacht, followed by a brilliantly orchestrated proposal. And yet, she felt the weight of it.

There was meaning in it.

The girl she'd been five years ago wouldn't have felt anything in those words. Would have found all of this dispassionate and unexciting.

The woman she'd become felt the binding quality of his vow down to her core.

"If you can promise the country what you've just promised me, I think your speech will be just fine," she said.

"I'm good with vows," he said slowly. "I kept my word to my brother for fifteen years. I devoted myself to my country. I gave aid when it was required. I never once saw my own pleasure above the safety of the nation. Unlike my brother, I am not a pleasure seeker. There is much more to life than that. When everything in a man's life is stripped away, the only thing he has left is his purpose. If a man has put his faith in things that burn, then when the fires of this world consume, there will be nothing left behind. But if a man puts his faith in rock, no matter how hot the blaze rages, it cannot be consumed. This country is my rock. If I am left with nothing else, I will fight for that to my dying breath."

Olivia looked to the intensity in his black eyes, and for just one moment she wished he could be speaking about her. Why couldn't someone treasure her that much?

You don't need that kind of ridiculousness. You don't need to depend on anyone.

She swallowed hard. "Say that. When you get up to speak, that's all you need to say. Yes, eventually policy will need to be addressed. But that can always be done with press releases. This nation is wounded, and I think those are the words that will heal it. You're the man who will heal it."

The man who might heal me.

The moment those words flitted through her mind she rebelled against them, panic fluttering in her breast like a terrified bird, raging at the cage of bone and flesh it was trapped in. She didn't want thoughts like that. She must be insane. Attaching some kind of emotional meaning to his words was foolish. Marcus had loved her, but he hadn't healed her.

Why do you suddenly think you need to be healed?

Really, her brain needed to calm down. Stop asking her questions she didn't have the answers to.

"I will simply have to trust you," he said.

"I'll do my best to make sure you don't regret that," she said, trying to lighten the mood.

His expression remained stone, and she wondered why she bothered to try to inject humor into any exchange with Tarek.

"I will do the same," he said finally.

"I have no doubt."

"I have procured a ring for you," he said after a small amount of hesitation.

Her heart scampered into her throat. "You have?" Why was she reacting to this? She was sitting in a man's office, in a very average day dress, about to be presented with a ring that was more the seal on a business agreement than anything else.

Her heart was pounding as though she was back on that yacht. With roses and champagne. A man that she loved.

She fought against the urge to close her eyes and turn away, because that would only make her look crazy. She was *being* crazy. Maybe because while this was a business arrangement in many ways, it was one that would involve sex. Closeness.

Only as much as you want.

That was what frightened her. How much *she* wanted.

He moved behind his desk, opening a drawer and producing a little box, placing it on the wooden surface.

She walked forward, pausing on the other side of the large piece of furniture. It stood between them, and for that she was grateful. Otherwise she might do something ridiculous, like touch him again. There really was no telling.

She reached out, touching the top of the jewelry box and sliding it toward herself. "Who chose this?"

"I did."

She looked at him, unbearably curious about what would make a man like him select a piece of jewelry over another. If it had anything to do with her, or with something else. It was like studying a rock wall for secrets.

And he wasn't going to tell her. Of course he wasn't.

She picked up the ring box and opened it slowly.

Her indrawn breath settled in the back of her throat, never making it all the way to her lungs. It was a simple ring, with a large square-cut stone the color of the crystal-blue water in the pristine lakes found in Alansund. An oasis in this desert. She couldn't help but see it that way.

She had removed her engagement ring and wedding

band before leaving Alansund, because there was no point wearing them when she was anticipating wearing another man's ring. Still, the idea of putting on one that was so different in style was both strange and a relief.

She wanted to ask him why. Why this ring?

But she didn't.

Instead, she took it out of the box without ceremony and slipped it onto the fourth finger of her left hand. "Even fits," she said.

"An accident."

"Or a sign," she said.

"If you believe in such things."

"I suppose," she replied. The man was impenetrable. And he refused to allow her to form a connection, no matter how small.

"There is much to prepare before the party." His forehead wrinkled. "I cannot quite fathom that I am attending a party."

She couldn't help but laugh, and it was a relief. There'd been too much tension inside her. "I can see that you aren't the most party oriented of men."

"I don't know how to have fun," he said, sounding completely mystified by the concept.

A scene flashed through her mind, unbidden, of her hands moving over his bare back, her legs wrapped around his hips as he drove in deep. That, she had a feeling, would be fun. She swallowed hard. "I'm sure you know some ways. Or at least some ways to relieve stress."

"I am fond of spending a few hours a day doing drills with my sword."

She blinked, biting the inside of her cheek. "Is that a euphemism?"

"I am speaking of an actual sword. What were you thinking?"

Her face got hot. "Nothing."

"I often feel we are speaking a different language sometimes."

"That could be because we're usually speaking your second language."

"I do not think that's it," he said, his black eyes intense on hers.

She sensed it was her opportunity to push for information, but she withdrew. Because she was tired of pressing only to be pushed away.

"It's a beautiful ring anyway. See, you did that well. No language barriers." She determinedly lightened things.

"It will send the proper message, one hopes," he said. "That we are moving forward unified, as a couple. For the sake of the nation."

"I think it will. I will handle coordinating the staff to organize the menu planning, music, things like that. You just focus on…smiling when people smile at you."

He put his hands into his pockets and he smiled. It was the saddest attempt at the facial expression she had ever seen. She found herself helpless to do anything but smile right back. And in that moment, the twist of his lips changed into something much more genuine. And her heart fluttered.

"Good," she said, the word tight, rushed. "Very good. You're going to be fine. All of this will be fine."

She wasn't sure if she was saying it for his benefit or for her own.

CHAPTER SEVEN

THIS WAS HER DOMAIN. Not the empty, echoing corridors. Not the feeling of being shrouded in a tomb. But this ballroom, glittering, full of people. An excuse to wear one of her beautiful custom-made gowns that had often been front-page news around the world when she was queen in Alansund.

The ballroom here in Tahar was different. With a high, domed ceiling, ornate golden detail and gems set ablaze by the lights suspended above. Everything was done up to perfection, and uniquely reflected Tahar and its beauty.

She was at ease here. But it was clear Tarek wasn't.

Tarek was solid stone beneath her fingertips. Were it not for the heat radiating from his body, she would have thought he'd calcified entirely. Obviously, while this might be her comfort zone, it wasn't his. She had expected as much, but she'd also had the feeling that there would be no preparing him for the moment. He simply had to live it.

She felt strangely protective of him. Odd, because she knew for a fact there was not a single person in this room he could not neutralize physically. But this wasn't his battlefield. Social settings, the thrust and parry, the sneak attack that came with a tongue and not a sword, were where she was most deadly. And she stood by, ready to defend.

She sneaked a sideways glance at him and her stomach tightened with unmistakable desire. There was no use pretending it was anything else. He was beautiful. That thought had scrolled through her mind often over the past few days.

His hair reached the top of his collar, curling slightly, but adding no softness to the shape of his face. His square, blunt jaw was so tempting to touch. She wanted to press her lips just beneath it, on his neck, right where his pulse beat, steady and hard.

When they were married, she would have that right.

A sliver of ice slipped through her veins, a shiver working its way along behind it.

She wasn't sure at all if he wanted her. She couldn't read him, the beautiful rock wall of a man. Perversely, that only made her want to rail harder against him. To try to force a crack.

But she knew better than that. Creating conflict was overrated.

So many people talked about speaking your mind. Standing up for yourself. What was the worst that could happen, and all that.

She knew.

The worst that could happen was you laid yourself bare before the people you loved most and they stared blankly back. Offering nothing. Giving nothing.

She couldn't think about that. Not now. Not when so much was going on around them. Not with members of international press stopping them to try to get Tarek to speak. Not with diplomats, politicians, social-program coordinators and businessmen all jockeying for Tarek's attention while he grew increasingly tense beneath her fingertips.

This was the physical representation of the paperwork that stacked up on his desk every day. The verbal version of the written requests he had to process constantly while being so unfamiliar with the task.

With the added issue of the media being in attendance, watching his every move.

She wondered if Tarek knew how vicious the press could be. He was very closed off about exactly what had transpired over the past fifteen years. But it was clear he had spent his time away from civilization almost entirely.

He wasn't familiar with computers, nor any modern conveniences. She wasn't certain whether or not he could drive a car. She didn't know if he'd ever faced the media before.

Another army that could be more vicious than one carrying weapons.

Tarek was making the official announcement about their engagement during his speech. And she had felt it would be best for them to open the evening with the speech. That way, people wouldn't be needling him for information beforehand. At least, that was the idea.

Also, she was afraid that the anticipation would be nothing more than a slow painful death for her. Maybe she was projecting her concern on to him. Especially as he seemed as immovable as ever.

But then, with him it was impossible to tell.

Either he felt less than the average man, really and truly, or he simply buried it deeper beneath the surface.

She imagined it was the latter, but she wasn't sure even he knew that.

In response to that thought, she let her hands drift over his forearm, and she felt him tense beneath her touch. Still, his expression remained the same.

"Are you ready to give your speech?"

"Yes," he said. There was no uncertainty in him. It went a long way in calming her riotous nerves.

"Good."

"What would you have done if I had said I wasn't ready?" he asked, and if she didn't know better, she would be certain there was a note of amusement in his voice.

"I would have rushed the front of the room and created a diversion so you could escape," she said.

"Would you have made the speech for me?"

"If not that, perhaps I would've done an interpretive dance."

The ghost of a smile toyed with the edges of his lips. "I cannot imagine that."

"Liar. If you weren't imagining it, you wouldn't be smiling."

"Did I smile?"

"Yes," she said. Warmth bloomed in her chest, spreading down to her stomach.

She had been so excited to have the room filled with people only moments ago, and now she wished they would all go away. All the better to focus on Tarek.

The ache she felt, the intense desire to know him, had only grown over the past week. And unfortunately she had found very little to satisfy it.

"I do not know any of these people," he said, looking around.

"I recognize a few of them," she said.

She hadn't made it public that she would be in attendance. In fact, she had called Anton and requested that he keep any connection between herself and Tarek secret. Things hadn't been certain, and she didn't want rumors preceding certainty.

Though tonight he would make the announcement. Tonight there would be certainty. She would have a place again.

"Who?" he asked.

"Well," she said, "Miranda Holt is a reporter. She covers a lot of society things in the States. I've known her for years. She used to attend gatherings my family would throw." By gatherings she meant grand galas. But details weren't important. "And over there is the ambassador of

Alansund and her husband. Others I know from their attendance at various functions there."

"Do you suppose they think it odd you're here with me?"

"I'm sure they are curious."

"Are you afraid they'll think you are betraying your husband's memory?"

His words burned for some reason. "It's been two years."

"But people think of you with him. Not with me."

"That will change."

"And what about you?" he asked. "Do you still think of yourself as being with him?"

It was a strange question. Tarek never seemed possessive of her. He seemed indifferent to her when he wasn't working directly with her on a project, so why he would ask something like that of her now she couldn't fathom.

It was personal, and his interest in her was nothing like personal.

She had to linger over the question. As she did, a strange sensation washed over her. "I don't," she said, the words soft. "Marcus and I lived very separate lives. We were…a team in many ways. But I can't claim a link with him that transcends the grave."

"You smile when you think of him," Tarek said, and if she didn't know better she might imagine that he was jealous.

"He gave me a lot of things to smile about."

That much was true. But suddenly, standing there, she had to acknowledge the gulf that had stood between herself and her husband. Had to acknowledge it because she felt it so keenly now. They had been two people walking side by side, toward a common goal. But their lives had not been intertwined. Losing him had left her cold, grieving. She had lost a cherished companion. But she had not lost a part of herself.

"A testament to the man," Tarek said. "I imagine you did not have to teach him how to smile."

Her heart twisted. "No. Marcus smiled easily. He was smiling when I walked into his life, and I daresay he was smiling when he went out of his own. He enjoyed the things of this world." He had taught her to enjoy them, as well. Had made her feel not half so lonely. The thought of him would always make her heart warm. "He also prized his independence, and as I very much prize mine, I had no trouble giving it to him." And if there were questions about what he did in his spare time, and whose bed he might be in when he wasn't in hers, she had never asked them.

She felt disloyal thinking about it now. Because she had never made an issue of it when he was alive, so she had no call to let those suspicions fester in his death. Even if he hadn't been faithful, she had never demanded him to be. And he had never made her unhappy.

She had not given him all of herself, so she could hardly expect him to give all of himself.

This was the wrong time to be having this realization. The wrong time to do any serious postmortem on her first marriage. Really, there was no right time. There was nothing left to fix. And she had been happy in her life, so thinking about fixing something that she had never thought broken was foolish indeed.

She'd never wanted to examine the cracks. Never wanted to pause for a state of the union for fear that, just as her parents had done, Marcus would do nothing but look at her with blank eyes and say, "There isn't anything more I can give."

"Marcus sounds a much easier man than I am. It isn't too late for you to turn back."

"Still so eager to get rid of me?"

"No," he said. "But I fear you have walked into this without fully understanding all you have to contend with."

"Maybe. But I'm not weak. And yes, you're different than he was. But…I am not looking to replace him. Not in the way you might think. I'm not looking to re-create our life together. I'm looking for something new."

"I quite like the idea that I am different," he said, and his words sent a little shiver of pleasure through her.

She wasn't sure why. Why she quite liked the idea of him being jealous. Of him wanting something from her. Or maybe she did, and she simply didn't want to examine it.

"I like the idea that you are not wholly at ease with everything happening. Oftentimes you seem far too confident, as though you are walking a trail you have blazed before. While the landscape remains entirely unfamiliar to me."

"Rest assured, Tarek, knowing royalty, knowing men, does not make you less of a mystery to me."

"I find this perversely pleasing." Something about the way he said the words lit her up inside, thousands of stars glimmering in the darkness that hadn't been there before.

"Since you find very little pleasing, perverse or not, I'm going to mark that in the win column."

"Do you have a win column?"

She nodded slowly. "I'm thinking of making one."

He looked her over slowly, his dark eyes assessing. "Put that dress in it."

And with that, he stepped away from her, cutting a swath through the crowd as he made his way toward the front of the room. And she was left standing there, barely able to breathe. What was it about that curt, barely a compliment that sent a wave of delight through her? She had been on the receiving end of some truly poetic words of praise. These were not poetic words in the least. And he had beat a hasty retreat after.

Perhaps, much like his smiles, they felt larger than they were because they were so hard-won.

He walked up the stairs to the podium that was set on the stage and her heart stopped. This was it. He looked completely calm, completely prepared. And she felt as if all of the nerves he should be feeling had been dropped down into the pit of her stomach, making it impossible for her to breathe.

She clasped her hands in front of her and whispered a prayer. Then she whispered it again. And again. She wanted him to succeed. She needed him to succeed. Needed both of them to succeed in this. This mattered so much, and she wasn't quite sure when that had happened.

He opened his mouth and began to speak. And he stole her breath.

Tarek's words flowed over her like warm honey. He was so cultured, so well-spoken, those words he had clung to in the lonely years in the desert well chosen, well guarded. She wondered if, in this case, it was a bit like preserving beautiful artifacts. If those words, so rarely handled, so rarely brought out before the world, were all the more precious and awe-inspiring for it.

Everyone in the room had the sense for it, she could see. They clung to each syllable as though it was gold.

"I know I am the brother you never saw," Tarek was saying now, "but you will see me now. I spent long years in the desert offering protection to our nation's borders. I will offer protection now. Not only in the shoring up of the borders, but in reaching beyond them. Tahar has been isolated for too long. We have been isolated for too long. I am deeply regretful for any crimes committed against our people, brought about by those in my bloodline. As for myself, I only know one thing. And that is how to protect. I will do so now. As for the other tasks required of a ruler, I am hopelessly outmatched. But I am fortunate enough to have found help. Queen Olivia, who served her country with her late husband, is to be my wife. She will be Sheikha of Tahar, and all that she gave to Alansund she will now give here. Our goal is to help each other by strengthening any weak points the other might have. With that goal, we will strengthen this country. I understand that you, here in this room and listening at home, might feel reason to distrust me. I understand that I will have to earn your allegiance. But I stand prepared to do that. I must prove myself, and I am willing. Thank you."

With that, he strode from the stage, his focus trained on her, his posture rigid, his gaze unflinching. As though he was completely oblivious to the thunderous applause happening around him. As though he had no sense of how well he had done.

In this sea of people, he stood alone. Nothing could break through. She wondered what it would take to reach him, to break down the wall.

She began to walk toward him, her heart thundering, the sound around her muted now. She stopped in his path and he continued on, his dark eyes blazing. And for just one moment she felt as if she was at least seeing behind the wall. Even if she still couldn't reach him, she was seeing more. The view beyond the rock and stone.

He paused in front of her and she reached up, putting both of her hands on his cheeks. "You were amazing," she said, keeping her eyes locked with his.

He let out a hard breath, and she could feel his relief resonating inside her. "I have not caused a war," he said. "Yet."

She heard the click of cameras, knew this moment was being captured on film. It would be a headline tomorrow. Her, and her peacock-blue gown, holding on to his face. It would look like love. It would at least look like lust.

Honestly, it was the second. On her end, at least.

Either way, it would make for a good headline. The kind of headline they wanted. Now, though, it was time for them to make the rounds. Time to be social. She had promised she wouldn't expect him to dance, but that meant that he didn't have a good chance at escaping social responsibilities.

Over the course of the next two hours she did her best to provide balance to Tarek's rather sullen version of conversation. She knew he didn't come across as humorless on purpose; rather, it was just who he was. She wasn't certain he was humorless per se, just that he didn't know how to express his humor with any effusiveness. Still, he came across as quite deadpan, and by the end of the evening she was exhausted trying to add some buoyancy.

And she felt even more determined to tear down that wall. It was almost as though he was operating on a separate plane. Possibly the plane he had been actively existing in the night she had seen him in the hall, naked and fighting imaginary enemies. There was strength there, vibrancy. Passion. She was hungry for it. To release it.

He had admitted to feeling off balance because she seemed so comfortable in her role. But he made her feel even more off balance. Because he was untouchable. And she, most certainly, was not. He had reached inside her early on, and she had not felt right since.

She knew that the party would go on for a while yet, and yet she also sensed that Tarek wouldn't want to linger. They had done their rounds, done their duties, as far as she was concerned. And the press would be appeased. It made no sense to keep him in the ballroom past the expiration date of his social skills.

She sensed he would only become more impenetrable as the evening passed.

"Let us retire," she said.

"Is it the appropriate time?"

"It's fine. You're very busy. No one will expect you to stay until the room clears."

He leaned in, his lips close to her ear. "Am I very busy?"

Her body immediately applied a dual meaning to his words, sending a shaft of heat down low. "I could ensure that you are."

She could think of a great many ways the two of them could stay busy for a few solitary hours. Ways that would finally force him to meet her in the present. Ways that might show her the man beneath the control. Something raw, something elemental. Rather than all of this guarded, protected, *manufactured* civility.

She'd had too much of that. Enough to last a lifetime. Too much isolation. She was so tired of being lonely. So tired of being alone.

Suddenly she was tired down to her bones. Careful smiles; careful words. Nothing upsetting. Nothing too loud. No questions asked. No answers given. On either side. Her entire growing-up years had been spent that way, and then her marriage. She was so desperately sick of it.

He made no response to her offer, allowing her to lead him quickly and quietly from the ballroom. The early exit would spark innuendo for the article about the evening. And that, she imagined, would be a good thing, too. Giving the press, the public, a love story rather than a cold alliance to offer a throne to a displaced queen and help to a barely civilized sheikh. Already she would add humanity to him. Already her presence was a help.

Though at the moment she did not intend to let the published innuendo stand as fiction. She fully intended to reach this man once and for all. To forge a connection between the two of them.

She could feel the palace security staying in line with them. Likely ensuring they weren't followed or disturbed. The people around them sensed it as well, for they cleared a path, making their exit easy.

Once they were out of the ballroom, she began to slowly

move her fingertips along his forearm, her way of signaling intent.

She felt a slight tensing in his muscles, the barest hint of a response. Coming from him, it might as well have been an emphatic yes.

"Are you headed back to your quarters?" she asked, staring straight ahead.

"Yes," he answered.

Her heart thundered in her head. "Okay."

She walked with him, not releasing her hold on him, and he did not release his hold on her. She took that as a significant development. They were, of course, headed to the same wing of the palace. And he might not realize it yet, but she intended to head to the same room. To smash that wall. And maybe, just maybe, one inside herself, too.

She felt as if she was suffocating. Had the feeling both of them were. Drowning on land.

If she could just touch him. If they could touch each other.

They reached the door of his chamber and she paused with him. "Do you need any help with your suit?"

"I don't think so."

It didn't surprise her that he didn't immediately grab hold of the invitation. Subtlety was not his strength. She found that charming in a strange way. More and more as the days passed.

"Perhaps we can discuss your speech."

He gazed down at her, the expression in his eyes unknowable. "If you wish." He pushed the door open and she followed him in.

He took a seat on a lush divan that was placed against the back wall of his chamber, assuming that same arrogant posture she'd seen during their first meeting in his throne room. With his black tie, black jacket, crisp white shirt and tailored trousers, he was very close to looking civilized. She didn't like it. She didn't want him civilized. Didn't want him hidden by yet more trappings.

That need, the need to have him, became a living beast inside her, growled, urged her forward. She began to walk toward him, watched as his dark eyes assessed her, attempted to anticipate her next move. She lowered her hands to her sides, curling her fingers around the silken fabric of her skirt, tugging it upward, exposing her legs, her thighs, as she continued to close the distance between them.

Then she saw it. A black flame burning in the depths of his eyes, so close to their natural color it would've been easy to miss. But it was there, glimmering like an oil slick. He was not untouched. He was not unmoved.

She approached, still clutching her skirt, placing one knee on the edge of the divan next to his before leaning forward, raising her hand on the wall behind him. He remained motionless, his expression fathomless. But of course it was. That was what he did. In a room full of people, he remained untouched. When applause thundered around him, he reacted like a deaf man.

He didn't play the game. No subtle push and pull. And so this time she wouldn't stop until she had destroyed his defenses, because that was what it would take. She realized that now, with certainty.

She rested her other knee on the divan, astride him now, sliding forward so that his big body was between her thighs, his heat teasing her, tempting her. He was motionless, as he had been the other times she had touched him. Except for the day he had pressed her palm against his chest. But then he had pushed her away, and she had allowed it. She had stopped.

But this time, she wasn't going to stop at touching.

She lowered her head, angling slightly, pausing just before her mouth met his. Enjoying the moment. The pause before fantasy became reality.

He smelled like clean skin, the intimacy of the scent hitting her like a punch in the chest. It made her heart beat faster, made her ache. And it stole her last bit of restraint. She closed the remaining bit of distance, fusing her lips to his.

Heat exploded behind her eyelids, burst in her stomach. She hadn't expected this. Not this instant firestorm that rocked her down deep. She was supposed to be seducing him, but she felt as if the tables had flipped, and there would be no coming back.

His lips were firm, hot, and only just now did she realize, immobile.

She moved her hand, gripped the back of his head and deepened the kiss, tracing the seam of his mouth with her tongue, requesting entry.

Her only warning of his next actions came in the form of a feral growl that rumbled in his chest, vibrating against her lips before she found herself being moved, Tarek's arm was like an iron band around her waist as he stood, bringing her with him. He moved his hand, fingers buried deep in her hair, his grip so hard it was painful, pinpricks dotting her scalp as he tugged her head back.

With two long strides, he had her pressed against the wall, his hold still tight in her hair and around her waist, his body hard and hot against hers. His breathing was ragged, the look in his eyes that of a hunted animal. Desperate. Intense.

Her hands were trapped between their bodies, her palms against his chest. And she could feel his heart raging out of control.

He wasn't unreachable now. Not untouchable or protected. It was terrifying. And it was everything she'd been craving.

He lowered his head slowly, his nose brushing hers, the movement deliberate, unpracticed. She let her eyes flutter closed, waiting. The moment stretched on forever, a small taste of eternity dropped into the middle of time.

Then, finally, he ended it.

When his mouth met hers it was rough, deep and hard. His lips were unforgiving, his tongue boldly pushing between her lips, sliding against hers. This was so far outside her experience. So different from kisses exchanged with careful aristocrats and playboys.

This was not a seduction. This was what it meant to be taken.

And this was where any semblance of stability he had carried with him tonight ended. He was not a man now but a beast. His muscular chest pressed tightly against her breasts, the solid length of his arousal resting against her thigh.

The kiss was bruising, almost painful. The movement of it strange, uneven. It carried with it the desperate quality of a man finding an oasis in the desert, drinking water he'd been deprived of. Absent of skill and social concern. Just the long, frantic satisfaction of a drought that had gone on for too long.

She was being conquered in a fashion that bordered on violence, and the neglected, hollow places inside her allowed themselves to be filled by it.

She was at his mercy, trapped between his body and the wall, held fast to his grip. And she loved it. There was no fear of seeming needy now, because he was holding nothing back. Because he needed her, it wasn't half so terrifying to prove that she needed this, too. To expose her neediness. How could it be when he was demonstrating that he needed her, too?

She flexed her hips, shifting her position slightly to bring herself in line with his arousal. His grip on her hair tightened when she did, but he didn't push her away. Her hands were still pressed against his chest, and she used that position to take hold of his tie, to wrench it free of the knot and cast it to the floor. Then she moved on to the buttons on his dress shirt, undoing the top two before sliding her hand beneath the fabric. She'd touched his chest before, and every single time it was a revelation.

Even better now that he was kissing her while she touched him.

His teeth grazed her swollen mouth and she retaliated, closing her teeth over his bottom lip, earning another growl that shook his entire being.

No one had ever touched her like this. No one had ever kissed her like this. And she had never realized how much she needed it.

But she needed more already. Needed that perfectly tailored suit of his on the floor, needed to discard her beautiful gown so that there was nothing at all between them.

She was about to make a move to do just that when she found herself completely bereft of his presence. He had released his hold on her, moving away from her, pacing back and forth.

"Tarek…"

"This is unacceptable," he said.

The words hit her like an arrow to her heart. "No. It's perfectly acceptable. We are going to be married. It is not acceptable for you to be with anyone else," she said, stating a possessiveness she had never once spoken aloud to Marcus, unsure why she was doing it now. "So if not with me, then who is this acceptable with?" Her voice was trembling now, and she despised it. "And when?"

"You test my control," he said. "That is what I find unacceptable."

"What do you need control here for?"

"Control is nonnegotiable."

"In this room?" She gestured around them. "With me?" She pressed her hands against her chest.

"In every room. Always."

"I'm going to be your wife. You have never been married before, and I assume you've been with other women, so I can't imagine what the issue is."

"You are not my wife yet." His words were insistent. Maddeningly opaque.

"But I will be."

"And when we consummate, it will be then. And it will be in the proper order."

"Am I to understand that you object to the spontaneity of this?" She was just peeved now.

"Yes. Because I refuse to allow my body to dictate my actions."

"There is nothing wrong with this…"

"After the wedding."

"Perhaps I don't want to wait until after the wedding." She was feeling slightly ashamed of how hard she was pushing. But then, why should she not? This was to be her marriage, too. What she wanted was important. And she wanted him.

"I must maintain my focus. I cannot afford to be distracted."

"Tarek—"

"I can be ruled by nothing. My only master is this kingdom. I must do everything in my power to protect it. I have spent my life casting off earthly desires, and I will not give in to them now."

Somewhere in her lust-fogged brain, she tried to make sense of his words. Tried to figure out something to say next. But she couldn't.

"Get out," he said, "or I will leave and find somewhere else to sleep tonight."

"I'm not going to beg," she said, her tone wooden. "Nor am I going to violate your person against your will."

"Tonight went well. Do not let this ruin it."

She sucked in a sharp breath. "Do you know anything about women?"

"No," he said, his tone dark.

"If you did, then you would know that rejection is always going to cast a pall over the evening."

"I'm not rejecting you. I am marrying you."

She flung her arms wide. "Well, I'm the luckiest girl in the world."

"Why are you angry with me?"

"Because," she said, ignoring the tightening in her throat, "you hurt my feelings."

Oh, how she despised herself for that moment of honesty. Maybe he was right. Maybe she was too deep in this to see that she was letting it affect her judgment. Normally, she was much more like Tarek. Guarded. Holding back pieces of herself. Not allowing desire or a need for anything to dictate her actions.

Maybe he was right to be wary of this thing between them.

His dark brow furrowed. "How?"

"Because…I take it as…commentary on my appearance. On my appeal."

He let out a hoarse laugh. "There is nothing wrong with your appeal. That is the problem. I cannot allow your appeal to become bigger than my goals." His dark eyes dropped down to her lips. "I must never let my own desires become larger than the tasks I have to complete."

"Not even desiring your fiancée?"

"Nothing. Where would it end? You don't understand… My brother… He was driven entirely by his own desire. It was not limited to sexual need. But greed. For power, for money. It overtook him. And we carry the same blood. Where does it begin? And where does it end? I don't know the answer. I will give no foothold to that level of greed. None. Not even for you. I must keep my focus clearly set."

"But later…"

"It will be different. It will be in its place. Part of my obligations, and not merely a temptation."

"Am I a temptation?"

He clenched his teeth tightly, a muscle in his jaw twitching. "You are the only real temptation I have ever faced." With that, he turned away from her, summarily dismissing her without another word.

But he couldn't dismiss the admission. She was a temptation for him.

She had never been a temptation for anyone before. For Marcus, she had been another indulgence in a lifetime of them. And she hadn't even truly been that. She had been the suitable woman, the one he had married.

She tempted Tarek.

She wanted to hold that close, to examine it and turn it over in private, where she could decide how exactly she felt about it.

"When exactly are we to be married?"

Another raw laugh escaped his lips. "From where I am standing, I would say the sooner the better."

CHAPTER EIGHT

A WEEK SINCE his encounter with Olivia had done nothing to cool the arousal in his blood. She tempted him, she tempted him beyond the need for anything else. He had been in dire straits in the desert. Sometimes without food, sometimes without water. And yet, now he craved her more than he craved either of those things. And it was unacceptable.

He was determined not to succumb to this. This wild need that was like a prowling animal inside him, tearing at years of well-practiced restraint.

Even now, he could taste her on his lips. Could recall exactly the soft, delicate feel of her mouth beneath his.

He had nearly crushed her beneath his need. He had been rough. He despised himself for that. For his lack of restraint.

He paced the length of his chamber. He had set the wedding day today. Had told his advisor that everything would need to be planned and set into motion for a ceremony to take place in two weeks' time. He'd had a notice sent to Olivia. He imagined she would be quite annoyed with him.

He didn't care. He was quite annoyed with her.

With all that she made him feel.

She expected sex. Of course she did. She had been married before, and she had no reason to expect their relationship to deviate from what she considered normal.

Nothing about him was normal.

He considered himself the furthest thing from an innocent. After all, he had endured grief, loss, torture. He had
taken the lives of enemies when necessary. There was no
place for innocence when you had watched a man's soul
depart from his body at your own hand. No, no room for
it at all.

And yet, while he considered himself devoid of innocence, the word *virgin* hung large as an accurate descrip-
tion for his state of being. Indeed, he had never even kissed
a woman until that moment with Olivia. There had never
been opportunity. Or perhaps there had been. There had
been many women in the Bedouin camps, widows who
probably would have appreciated a bit of comfort and company. But he had never allowed his focus to stray. Had never
allowed the impulses of his body to control his actions.

That focus, that determination had been paramount to
his survival. Releasing his hold on it was never an option.

Whether he was a virgin or not had never mattered
until now. Sexual desire was simply another appetite he'd
cast off.

But he was discovering that introducing the desire for
sex, the appetite for it, was much different than an appetite
for food. He had managed to find ways to keep himself
fed without allowing himself to desire rich flavors. Without allowing himself to be controlled by specific cravings.

Now that he had tasted Olivia, he wondered if there
was any way to satisfy sexual need in a basic way. One
that wouldn't consume.

He doubted it now.

Of course, part of the issue was that he remained un-
educated on the subject.

He had seen a great many animals copulate. Knew what
that looked like. Knew the mechanics. And yet, the way
Olivia looked at him, the way she responded to his touch,
the way he had watched his brother abandon all for the

sake of hedonistic appetites, told him that there was much
more to it than that.

And beyond that, the gnawing hunger that had taken
residence inside him from the moment he had first seen
Olivia told him there was more.

Preparation. That was what always helped a new soldier. Doing drills, learning everything there was to know
about the enemy.

Preparation made events seem less remarkable.

Of course, there was no way for him to acquire physical
practice. But when practical experience couldn't be had,
reading would suffice.

He walked across the room to the vast library housed
in the other end of the chamber, certain there was a book
here that would satisfy his curiosity. After all, his brother
had purchased a great many of the books.

His brother had been a bit shorter than he was, so Tarek
looked slightly lower than eye level scanning the center
shelves for anything that seemed to pertain to the subject.
He was not disappointed.

He opened the volume, his eye immediately drawn to
the detailed sketches of anatomy on the first pages. Yes, he
could see he had a great deal to learn. He turned the page
and there was a drawing of a man caressing a woman's
bare breasts. He thought of Olivia, the way she had felt
pressed against his body. The soft, feminine shape of her
and how she had fitted so perfectly against him.

Need bloomed hot and low in his stomach.

In that moment, he had a great many of his own fan-
tasies. But he wanted to know all of the possibilities. He
wanted to miss nothing.

He squashed that thought. This wasn't about him. It
was about her. Fulfilling his obligations as a husband and
nothing more.

More important even than fulfilling obligations was

mastering his need. He must form a strategy so that when faced with his opponent, he would not waver.

She was so soft. And his hands, warrior's hands, so rough. When he placed them over her body he had to be sure he would deliver only pleasure. Had to be certain he would not…break her.

Of course he knew the mechanics of sex. He'd been fifteen when he'd left the palace after all. But fifteen-year-old boys might nudge each other and talk about women's bodies. But they did not discuss a woman's pleasure. Did not discuss control.

He needed to understand both of those things. For Olivia had known the touch of another man. She deserved pleasure.

And he required control.

An hour later, he had made it halfway through the book and was not feeling at all like education had done anything to lessen his desire. Certainly, he had some ideas that were new. And very, very interesting.

But that had not been the plan.

There was a firm knock on his door, and he cast the book aside. Strange that this was something he felt the need to hide, but he did. He hated needing to admit his lack of mastery.

He stood, ignoring the vague ache in his groin and the tightness in his stomach as he made his way to the door.

He opened the door only to meet Olivia's fearsome blue gaze. "Yes?"

"I am informed, by a member of staff, by the way, not you, that we are to be married in two weeks."

"Yes," he bit out.

He would not allow her entry. His head was entirely filled with the images in that book and the images painted by the explicit instructions. And if he allowed her to get too close, he would only be tempted to put his new education to practical use.

"That's impossible. It takes months to plan an event of that magnitude. You forget, I have been through this before."

Yes, she had. In this, and in the things he had just been researching, she had more experience than he did.

But he frightened people. And he found that was more effective than experience at times.

Not with sex, obviously, but in the planning of a wedding, yes.

"It is eminently possible. This will not be like your first wedding."

"Well, it couldn't be. Good luck getting five hundred live doves this late in the game."

"I cannot tell if you're joking or not."

"I'm not. My first wedding was ridiculous. Beautiful, but ridiculous."

"I cannot promise this wedding will be less ridiculous. Less extravagant, certainly."

"Two weeks?"

He arched a brow. "Did you want more time?"

She shook her head resolutely. "No. I am decided. But I'm doubtful that you can pull this off in two weeks."

"Why would you doubt? I have you to help."

"I can't decide if I feel complimented or put upon."

"Why choose one? You are a woman, and I'm quickly learning that means you can be both."

"You do learn quickly," she said.

He hoped so.

"Two weeks," he reiterated.

"Two weeks," she said. "But, Tarek, next time, tell me yourself when you set our wedding date."

He nodded, attempting a smile, because this, he was confident, was a joke of sorts. "Next time."

* * *

Two weeks passed quickly. Were Tarek a beloved monarch who had been on the throne for years, he could see the point of creating a spectacle out of his wedding. For the media, for the citizens. But as he was not, he felt there were better ways to spend his country's money than on a lavish event they had not chosen, and one he and Olivia certainly didn't need.

He had, in the past few weeks, spent time looking at photos of Olivia. It was easier than talking to her to gather information. Perhaps not the most up-front way of going about getting to know her, but he had been avoiding her since the kiss.

During that research he had seen photos of her at many social events. And he had seen her first husband. Polished, as blond as she was. He had seen their wedding. An intricate event that had lasted two days and commanded the attention of the media worldwide.

And then Tarek had seen pictures of her with himself. Mainly unsmiling, definitely not polished.

There was a photo of her holding his face, just after the speech. Her hands were so very pale on his dark skin. Highlighting the differences between them. She had said she did not think of herself as being part of her first husband still, and yet, looking at the pictures, he could see that she had been. They blended.

Whereas he…he did not look as if he belonged with her.

Of course, that was immaterial. They were marrying each other anyway. Today, in fact.

Which meant that tonight he would be out of excuses for not consummating the attraction between them. He gritted his teeth. They were not excuses. He had valid reasoning for resisting the heat that fired in his blood whenever she touched him. What he had said to her about his brother was true. Malik had been a man entirely ruled by his own desires. Tarek was a man made entirely of resistance. A man who had learned to shun everything unnecessary.

Seeing to his wife's physical needs now fell under the banner of his responsibility, he could not deny that. But giving in to temptation in his bedroom after the speech seemed a violation of everything he was.

He had wanted her then. Hard, and fast. He had known it would be fast.

Heat lashed him like a whip.

He was more prepared now than he had been then. He had read not just one, but several books on the subject. And he had learned a great deal about female anatomy. He was grateful that he had, because he'd had no idea just how intricate the mechanics of the act could be.

Neither had he anticipated just how much his body would be captivated with the promise of it.

He had spent thirty years denying his impulses. His needs.

The prospect of no longer denying certain impulses loomed large. The thought, the very idea, had worked its way under his skin like a bullet, traveling through his body, blooming outward slowly, looking for a place to land where it might destroy whatever it touched.

Not the most delightful analogy. But then, he wasn't surprised, considering he was rarely delightful.

Olivia's first husband had been delightful. All of Tarek's research had brought him to that conclusion. He wondered how quickly she would tire of being with a man who wasn't. Though he had not coerced her into this. Far from that. She had been the one to come to him. The one to present a case for why he needed her.

Not for the first time he wondered what she was getting out of this. If she had thought to replace what she had lost, to recapture what it was to be royalty, she had most certainly come to the wrong place. Her life in Alansund had been filled with parties, glittering affairs, delightful excursions on the lake, picnics with her husband, the king.

Tarek could honestly say he would not be engaging in any of that.

Sex, however, would not be something he denied her. He was ready now. Preparation always brought a clearer head. Now that he had a plan, he would remain in command of his body, of his impulses when the time came. And in that way, he was determined to please her. Because it certainly seemed more desirable than throwing an increased number of parties.

For a start, it only required there to be two of them in the room. For another thing, Olivia would be naked.

He could not deny that added incentive.

He ignored the tightening in his gut. He could not focus on that. He had to focus on getting through this day.

He turned and faced the mirror, tightening the black tie he wore. When given the option, he had chosen a Western-style suit for the day, seeing as he was marrying a Western woman. He had thought hard about it. Because he cared deeply for his people and for their traditions.

But in the end, it was Olivia he had dressed for.

He had no idea of what she might wear. Part and parcel to his avoidance of her, both in the past couple of weeks, and completely today, as she had informed him coolly during their last brief encounter, that it was bad luck for the groom to see the bride on the day of the wedding.

He had not told her then that he didn't believe in luck. Because she very clearly did, and he did not want to hurt her feelings again. He'd been very put out by the fact that he had. In addition to lacking sensibilities, Tarek also imagined that he lacked feelings. His soft, pretty fiancée most certainly possessed more than he did.

Naturally, he did not know how to consider them, as nothing inside him reflected her internal workings. Which meant he would simply have to watch. And he would have to try. He could not trust his dealings with the woman to be intuitive.

The door to his chamber opened slowly and his advisor appeared. "It is time, my sheikh."

For the first time in memory, Sheikh Tarek al-Khalij felt fear. For today, he would not face down an enemy, but a bride. His bride.

However, much like an enemy attack, it was not something that could be waylaid.

"I am ready."

Olivia adjusted her heavy veil, trying to quiet the pounding of her heart she readied herself to walk down the aisle. To pledge herself to a man she still felt she barely knew.

Strange that she was so conscious of that with Tarek. She had to confess, standing there now in her ornate gold-and-white gown, that she wasn't entirely certain she and Marcus had known each other any better.

What Tarek lacked was the ability to let those around him see just enough that they might be fooled into thinking they knew him. She and Marcus had shared certain things freely. Smiles, their bodies, small talk. Easy conversation. Neither of them ever asked difficult questions. Neither of them had ever asked questions at all.

She shoved that thought aside. This was not the time to think about Marcus.

Though, really, it was inevitable that she would. Think about the other man who had been her husband on the day she was ready to marry another. Maybe, if she was in love with Tarek, she wouldn't.

As it was, it was difficult not to draw comparison. To grasp at something to make the situation feel less foreign. To recall her other wedding day in an attempt to make this one feel less significant. It was a cheap trick that even she saw through, and yet, that wouldn't stop her from trying it.

She caught sight of her reflection in the mirror, and her heart sank down low. This was so different in every way. There was no way she could use the fact that this was her second wedding to calm her nerves. If anything, highlighting the differences between the two only made this feel more terrifying.

She recalled the bespoke gown she'd worn the first time. It had made headlines around the world. Had set a trend for weddings for the next year.

This gown was weighted down with the tradition of the nation. Long sleeves, intricate embroidery, a thick belt just beneath her breasts, also gold. In so many ways the difference in gown symbolized the difference between the two unions. The other, light, showy, focused on the couple. This one heavy. Focused squarely on the need of Tahar.

And of yourself. Let's not start pretending you're too altruistic.

All right, she wouldn't pretend she was being completely selfless. She quite wanted a place in life. A little bit of security. A purpose.

And then there was…him.

She was so attracted to him. But now that sleeping with him wasn't a spontaneous thing, she found she was quite nervous about it. Now it was the finish line to a marathon of the day, and that put it in a slightly different light than the natural progression of a kiss, or a touch.

Also in keeping with the theme. Everything concerning Tarek was weighty.

"Sheikha?"

Olivia turned, surprised that Melia was already addressing her as such. The servant inclined her head, betraying no nerves in spite of the import of the event.

"They are ready for you."

Olivia nodded, wishing she had opted to carry a bouquet. Something, anything to do with her hands.

Alas, she had nothing. So she gripped the front of her skirt, lifting it slightly as she walked through the halls toward the small sanctuary that was in a different wing of the palace.

Her throat suddenly grew tight, a pulse beating in her head. She had to close her eyes against it.

She had no connections in there. Her parents…well, they weren't coming. Not a huge surprise, but the phone call last night had still left her nearly hollow with pain.

Emily wasn't well. Emily couldn't stand the heat and the dust. It was hardly fair to leave her…

And Olivia had said she understood, of course, because it was all she had said for years.

Only once had she fought back.

Her fifteenth birthday. She'd told them she would make the cake; she would make dinner. They just had to be there.

But they hadn't been. Because Emily had been hospitalized and they'd visited her instead. And she'd been so angry. They'd stayed with Emily all evening. She'd been broken over it. Something in her shattering that had never quite been repaired after.

When she breathed in too deeply, she swore she could still feel it. Lodged like a barb deep in her chest.

How dare you miss this? I asked for this. Just this!

It isn't as though we want your sister bedridden in a hospital, Olivia. Have some sensitivity. You will have all of your birthdays. You'll grow up. You'll marry. What will Emily have? How long does she have?

They'd been right. And whatever she'd been feeling… She hadn't had any right. And as isolated as she'd felt before she'd poured her emotions out in front of her mother and father, she'd felt even more so after.

Because when they looked at her after that, all they

saw was her selfishness. They had an ill daughter. They'd needed her to carry the weight. To be as happy and self-contained as she could be, and she'd failed.

She'd stepped outside her position, and after that had found no place at all.

Olivia swallowed hard.

She faced a room empty of her own connections. The only person there she knew would be the man she was pledging her life to, and as she had only just been thinking, she barely knew him.

The ornate doors to the sanctuary were closed, and Olivia paused in front of them, waiting for them to swing open, as she knew they would. She had discussed this briefly with the wedding coordinator. She knew already there would be very few people in attendance. Nobility, members of the Bedouin tribes, a few approved members of the press and palace staff. It would be nothing like that first wedding with thousands of attendees, where the world had been watching.

But there had been something insulating about that. So many people it had seemed surreal. They had all blended into one.

She had been floating on a cloud that day, insulated by her happiness. There was no insulation today. Only the stark reality of the cold stone walls around her and the imposing doors in front of her.

Doors that suddenly parted, revealing the small crowd, and the man that she was meant to bind herself to.

What surprised her was how immediately everyone else faded. Her eyes were locked on Tarek. He owned her focus, her attention. He was the reason she took that first step forward, and the next. She was certain of this, she realized, looking at him. But this wasn't the giddy certainty of a girl imagining she had finally found that sense of love and belonging she had always fantasized about. This was different.

He was different.

She locked eyes with him, drawn ever nearer by the black flame burning there. He was magnificent. A modern-day warrior born of the desert sand. He was strength personified. And yet again, he was in one of those maddening, perfectly tailored suits that made a mockery of the entire concept of civility. Showed it for what it was. A cloak, a weakness. A construct used by those too frightened to reveal their true selves.

That was, she realized in that moment, one of the things she admired most about Tarek. He did not hide himself. She doubted he even knew how.

She arrived at the front of the room, and the clergyman presiding over the ceremony began to speak in Arabic. She had only a base understanding of the language, allowing the words to wash over her in a wave, the gist of them penetrating, but not the fine meaning. She had read a transcript of what would be said today, so she had a fair idea of what would be asked of her in terms of vows, of what those in attendance were hearing now.

She would have to learn her new language. Would have to become a part of this nation as she had become part of Alansund.

In many ways, she felt it had already become a part of her. She felt the change.

She repeated her vows slowly, in the phonetic Arabic she had memorized while reading the ceremony, with help from Melia. She kept her eyes focused on the ground as she did, her lungs tight, growing tighter still whenever she looked up and met Tarek's gaze.

When she finished speaking, it was his turn.

But he did not repeat the vows they had learned. And he did not speak in Arabic.

"I am a man of the sword," he said slowly, the grave intent in his words drawing her focus upward. "And I now pledge this blade to you. I will empty my veins before I allow one drop of your blood to be spilled. You are one of mine now, as this country is mine. And I will give all to defend and protect, and to destroy any who should seek to destroy you. Just as you belong to me, now I belong to you. I pledge my loyalty, my body, to yours. And never will I share what is meant to belong to us with any other. I shall honor your gift, the gift you give of yourself, and never misuse it. I have sworn to protect, to uphold the honor this country was founded on. Thus, I shall protect you. Thus, shall I treat you with the highest honor."

He reached out and took her hand in his. She was conscious of how small, how pale it looked, concealed entirely by his. He held her tightly, his black eyes never leaving hers, cementing the vow, one she felt all the way down to her soul.

Suddenly her promises seemed so shallow. So empty. What had she done but repeat words spoken to her? Words she barely understood.

That was very like her first marriage.

A marriage where she had chosen the thinnest facade of connection over any sort of true intimacy and all the deep, exposing terror that came with it.

So she'd stayed on the surface. And she was ashamed now in the face of his sincerity.

What Tarek had said, those were vows. A pledge from the depth of his being.

She was honored. She was not worthy.

But she wanted it. Wanted it with a ferocity that shocked her.

Maybe it was time to stop being shocked by how many feelings Tarek seemed to call out of her with effortless ease.

Then he released her, and as a blessing was pronounced

on them she found herself being led back down the aisle she had just come up, all eyes in the room on them, somber expressions all around. She'd been told to expect that, too. The reception would be the place for festivities. This ceremony was treated with all seriousness.

When they exited the sanctuary, Melia was waiting for them.

"The feast will be served in the grand hall," she said. "If you go there now, you can take your seats and await the celebrations."

Olivia took hold of Tarek's hand and they started to walk down the corridor together. A sense of belonging filled her. She looked to the side, at the man who had become her husband, and her heart felt as if it had grown two sizes. This was something deeper. Something more.

The sort of thing she'd been afraid to reach for all these years. Right here. Right beside her.

He looked at her, his brow raised. "Yes?"

"Just letting it sink in."

"That we are married?"

"Yes. That this is my home. That you're my husband. All of it."

He stopped, taking hold of her other hand and turning her so that she was standing facing him, his expression fierce. "Why? What is it you want? I spent the past two weeks looking at pictures of your old life and Alansund."

Her stomach tightened. "Why?"

"To understand you."

"You could have spoken to me."

He lifted a shoulder, dismissing her words. "The photographs I looked at conveyed much. And so I'm curious, why would you leave all of that to come here?"

Her throat constricted, making words all but impossible. "Because it isn't there anymore. There is no place for me. I know we haven't had a chance to talk about this. I don't…I don't like to talk about the past. I don't have a lot of happy things there."

He raised his brows, his dark eyes full of something… understanding, maybe? Which was so strange she could hardly stand it. "I have some idea of what that might be like. Will you tell me?"

"My sister was ill. She is ill. She's had a terrible auto-immune disease since we were children. My parents spent years of their lives in hospitals. Even now, she's very fragile. Truthfully, she's lucky to have lived as long as she has. But that meant that my life was solitary. Very often I was at home while they attended clinical trials. While Emily was hospitalized. It's just one reason I felt so suited to palace life. The house was always full. I quite like that. And Marcus had a way of making everything feel easy. Fun. Bright. I didn't have much experience of that. I'm afraid of being alone. I don't like it. I don't like feeling displaced. Like I'm an incidental. Because I've had too much of it.

"Emily can't help it. I hate even saying any of this. It isn't her fault. It isn't my parents' fault. And I found a way to fix all of that. It's just that…Marcus died. And there isn't a place for me there anymore, and it's nothing but that yawning, horrible feeling of being extra. I tried to… There was this man who was a diplomat for Alansund and I tried to make things work with him, but it barely got past hello. I felt… I hate feeling like I failed in my duty. Like I didn't hold up my end."

She thought of that horrible moment. The birthday party. When she'd yelled at her parents for not caring. When they'd looked at her as though she'd failed in her unspoken duty. To be content with neglect, because she had health. She had never felt so broken. "So when Anton suggested this as a solution, I jumped at it. That's why I'm here. At least here I matter."

She couldn't quite fathom why all of that had come

spilling out. She had never even talked to Marcus about it like that. Oh, he had known about Emily's condition, but she had never spoken to him about how it made her feel.

But Marcus had never asked.

Tarek put his hand on her cheek, the gesture so shocking she froze, her eyes wide. "You are needed. Know that."

With that, he lowered his hand, continuing to walk with her down the corridor. The ache in her chest deepened, widened, a crack in a wall she hadn't been aware of until recently.

She didn't have time to ponder it too deeply. They entered the dining hall to find it glowing from floor to ceiling. The chandeliers were lit; candelabras lined the room. Flowers wound around everything. There was nothing restrained about any of this. It was an explosion of joy, of color. And since Olivia couldn't muster up any of her own joy, she appreciated it blooming around her.

At the head of the low table were cushions in red, gold and blue, awaiting herself and Tarek.

"This is beautiful. I've never been to a party like this," she said.

It reminded her very much of that birthday party again. But people were here. And it was glittering and full. So she would focus on that.

"Nor have I."

She followed him to their positions, taking a seat beside him. Questions formed in her mind, hovering on her lips. She had just shared some of herself. And she wanted very much to try to get him to share his own experiences.

"How is that possible? Why were you out in the desert?"

Guests began filing into the room, more than had been in the ceremony. She had known this would be the case, too. There was also a feast outside the walls of the palace, food being given freely to the citizens of Tahar to celebrate the marriage of their sheikh.

Along with guests, musicians came in, music filling the space, echoing off the ceiling and the jeweled walls. In time with the music, platters of food came next, and her question was lost in the noise and shuffle.

She picked at a bit of spiced lamb on her plate, unable to muster up any appetite.

She looked over at Tarek, who was sitting with one leg curled beneath him and the other bent at the knee, his elbow resting on top of it as he made quick work of the food on his plate. He trained dark, serious eyes on her. "I was in the desert because my brother feared what I would become if I was here."

"What do you mean?"

"It was not until recently that I realized just who he was. What he was doing to our country. It was not until recently I realized that he was very likely the one who'd orchestrated the assassination of my parents."

His hard blank words hit her like bricks. One after the other. And she was barely able to recover from the first blow when a second arrived.

"I think he was afraid I would know. I think he was afraid of what I would do. So he broke my will. Filled my head with his teachings. His truths. Sent me away where I could be of no threat. To guard the borders. To protect his evil empire while he reduced it to ash from within." He took another bite of food. "I have been slowly coming awake for years. Slowly coming into understanding." He looked at her, his gaze so cold it sent a shiver down her spine. "He turned me into a creature. Tortured me until I knew nothing but pain and his words. I am what I was made to be. I doubt I will ever be anything else."

CHAPTER NINE

THE REST OF the reception passed in a fog for Tarek. He had not intended to speak to Olivia with such honesty. He saw no point in infecting her with the darkness that lingered in his past. He scarcely saw the point of infecting himself with it. However, the longer he stayed here in the palace, the more he remembered. The more often he woke, naked and reaching for his sword, his entire body burning with memories of what it had been like to be subjected to the physical and emotional torture visited upon him by his own brother after the death of their parents. It had all been under the guise of strengthening him, but he saw it now for what it was.

The only thing that had gotten him through had been the vision of his people swimming before him. The idea that he might be the perfect weapon raised up to protect them. To prevent what had happened to his parents from ever happening again. It had not then occurred to him that the threat had come from within the palace. That it had been his own brother who had orchestrated their demise. He had only the scribbles of a prince in a private journal, and shattered pieces of memory that sometimes pushed to the fore, piercing his brain with painful, vivid replays of conversations he'd heard. As a boy? During his torture, he couldn't be sure. They were too broken.

And they were not what he intended to focus on now. But Olivia had shared pieces of herself with him, and he had felt obliged to do the same. Now, though, it was time for them to return to their chamber. It was time for them to become husband and wife in every sense of the word.

A sense he feared he still did not fully understand.

I am what I was made to be. I doubt I will ever be anything else.

His own words, the truth in them, reverberated through him as he and Olivia left the hall to raucous applause and cheers from the guests in attendance.

His body did not know how to feel pleasure. His hands did not know how to give it.

He thought back to the fantasy he'd had a week before, looking down at the book that had held so many secrets to sexual gratification. The fantasy of placing his hands on Olivia's breasts. Her skin was so soft, perfection, unmarred by the things of the world. His were scarred. His entire body was scarred. Rough. More weapon than man. How could he begin to touch her in a way that would bring her pleasure?

He would have to trust the mechanics. What he had learned in his study. Just as he had learned to trust that drills would suffice when wartime came. That some part of him, instinct, would rise up and take over, join in with what he had learned.

And yet, it seemed rather a large chance to take on such a delicate, easily crushed creature.

They walked on in silence, heading toward his chamber. Neither of them said anything; neither of them touched as they walked inside. Tarek closed the doors firmly behind them, and when he turned it was to see Olivia, slowly removing the bangles from her wrists. She placed the first one on the vanity with a decisive click, followed by a second, and a third. Until she had removed each ring of gold and silver from her arms.

Then she reached up, working small combs from her

hair, detaching the veil that had hung over her shoulders. She placed the beautifully adorned fabric across the top of the bangles, her eyes never leaving his.

"I have been thinking," she said, "about what you told me."

His stomach turned over. "I am sorry. It is nothing good to think about."

"Maybe it isn't. But it happened. I was thinking also about the vows you made to me during the ceremony."

"I know it was not what was written. But all of those things spoke of love, of clinging to one another. And I do not understand those things. But I understand protection. Possession. Perhaps neither are very romantic concepts, but they are real in my heart."

She nodded slowly. "I know. It made them meaningful. I understood. But it made me feel that I owed you something of the same. Not just words that were written for me by someone else. Not a traditional sentiment about marriage when nothing about this is traditional. When nothing about the two of us is traditional."

"And have you decided what they are?"

"I haven't rehearsed them. But… Yes. I have never been tortured, Tarek. I have never been alone the way that you have. I haven't known loss as you have done. I promise that when we touch my hands will bring you nothing but pleasure. I promise that I will never send you away. I promise that no matter how long it takes, I will make you see that you are not what he made you. You are a man. And I will do everything I can do to ensure you feel like one."

As she spoke the final words, her hands went to the belt on her dress, nimble fingers unhooking the tiny catches there, letting it fall free. Then she moved to the tiny buttons at the front of the gown, undoing each one with a kind of purpose that carried great weight.

She parted the fabric, opening the dress at the front and letting it slide from her shoulders, a silken river at her feet.

She was bare beneath the gown. And he couldn't breathe.

He had never in his life seen a naked woman in the flesh. Drawings, statues, paintings were useless renderings. They did not and could not capture the majesty of what he saw before him. He had to grit his teeth to try to maintain a grip on his control.

She was bathed in golden light, the soft halo provided by the candles in the room conforming to each curve and contour of her figure. He was transfixed by every part of her. The shadow of her collarbone, her round, full breasts, tipped with dusky, pale nipples. The slope of her waist that narrowed then widened again for lush hips and thighs. The dark shadow at the center holding his focus above all else.

She was, now and forever, the epitome of a woman to him. And for all of his days, this was the image he would see when the word was spoken.

Everything else, everyone else, was a pale shade in comparison with her.

"I think now we're past time for discussion," she said, luminous eyes meeting his. "Perhaps it's time we do something other than talk."

The book had not mentioned this. That he would scarcely be able to breathe. That he would be so hard it would be a physical pain. That his hands would shake. That he would be nearly immobilized with his desire, while also fighting the urge to pull her hard against his body, to lay her down and push deep inside her with no preliminaries whatsoever while he chased a release that was sure to surpass anything he had ever known before.

He thought that he had learned more than the mechanics. But he saw now that there was more still. And that theory would scarce be helpful here.

Because he had not taken into account what she might do. And what it might make him feel. He had made it all about her. Her pleasure. Meeting her expectations of the husband so that he would not be remiss in his responsibilities.

He had fancied his own control so iron that he needn't consider it.

He had been a fool. And now he was a fool standing before a naked woman.

She began to walk toward him, each step creating a slight wave through her soft body, her breasts keeping rhythm with each movement. She looked down, her eyes clearly following his own line of sight, then looked up at him, a slight smile curving her lips. "I'm glad you're pleased."

"Go to the bed," he said, his voice barely recognizable to his own ears. Though that wasn't unusual. Sometimes, out in the desert, he had gone long enough without speaking that when he did so again, it was a surprise.

Her shoulders stiffened, one pale brow arching. "I didn't realize you were one to give commands."

"Neither did I. Go to the bed."

He had to seize control here. There was no other option.

She turned away from him slowly, and he allowed himself a long moment to admire the view of her from behind. The enticing dimples low on her back just above the rounded curve of her bottom. The gentle sway of her hips as she walked away from him, complying with his demands.

Fire shot through his veins with a crack. This beautiful, fierce creature was obeying his commands. Soft, naked, lovelier than anything. Following his instruction. She had been the aggressor when it came to physical interaction between the two of them in the past. Tonight, the control would be his.

It was how it must be.

She sat on the edge of the mattress, her eyes watchful. "Lie back."

Her expression held many unspoken questions, but she complied. She breathed in deep, her breasts rising and falling. She was the picture of supplication, and yet he knew better. Because he knew Olivia.

"Raise your arms above your head," he said.

She complied with that, as well. He admired her ease with her body. Her lack of nerves. She had confidence in him. Of course, she didn't know the truth.

If things went well, she never would. It would be unnecessary.

He moved to the end of the bed, to a vantage point that provided him with an optimum view. Her legs hung over the edge of the bed, her knees pressed together, her eyes still on his. He took a step toward her, each step increasing the tightness in his chest, his difficulty in breathing. He paused at the edge of the mattress, leaning forward, pressing his hand into the soft bedding. Then he raised his other hand, tracing her cheekbone, the lovely curve of her upper lip, down to her chin. Her lids fluttered closed, her mouth relaxing, a sweet sigh escaping.

So his touch hadn't harmed her. Wasn't too rough.

He moved his fingertips across her throat and down lower between the valley of her perfect breasts. He watched as her nipples grew tighter, watched until the temptation to touch became too great. He let his fingers drift over her, brushing his fingertips over her sensitized skin. Satisfaction rocked him as she shivered, as he fulfilled that fantasy of his. She was softer than he had dared imagine. Softer than he had believed anything could be.

He let his exploration continue downward, stopping at the patch of curls between her thighs. He was shaking.

From the inside out. Faced now with the full brunt of the desire he had spent fifteen years suppressing.

He was not stone. He was a man. A man who greatly desired the woman before him. Desire such as this had been stripped from him, a necessity for his survival he had told himself. A necessity for his mission.

Protection. Against corruption, against distraction.

But now, with Olivia before him, all he could think was that he had been missing a part of himself, and it had been returned to him.

He almost feared touching her. Fear that he could not meet the need within her. That the need within her did not match his own. That he lacked the skill to bring her to satisfaction.

He knew he lacked skill. All he had was desire.

So he would give her that. All of it. Everything within him.

He pushed his fingers lower, and she gasped as he met with slick flesh. Her knees fell open, allowing him greater access. Heat rose in his face, his breath coming in hard, short bursts, his heart beating so hard he feared it might burst from his chest. He fought to maintain his control, to ignore the ache building between his own thighs.

He stroked her gently, closing his eyes and letting the pages of the book fill the space in his mind. He did exactly as those pages had instructed him to, touching her just where they had said. Using the evidence of her desire to ease the motions. She made sharp, soft noises, her stomach pitching with each breath. She raised her hips off the bed, pressing herself more firmly into his touch.

"Please," she whispered, "Tarek, please."

He didn't know what she was asking for. His mind went blank, the instructions he had placed there dissolving like sand through an hourglass.

She lowered her hand, placing it over his, pushing his

hand down farther, pressing his fingertip into the entrance of her body. He looked up, meeting her gaze. Her eyes were bright, the color in her cheeks high. She pressed her hips into his touch yet again, and he answered her silent request, pushing his finger deep inside her.

A harsh, raw sound was wrenched from her lips and he withdrew from her, afraid he had done something wrong.

"Don't," she said. "Don't stop."

She put her hand back over his, guiding him back to where he'd been.

He reclaimed his position, continuing to stroke her gently with his thumb as he entered her again.

She let out a shivering breath, his name on her lips. It struck him in the chest like an arrow, warmth spreading outward like blood. Arousal such as this felt like an injury. So acute it was almost pain. But beneath that, a deep, unending pleasure unlike anything he'd ever known. He knew the ultimate goal of something like this was climax, and yet he found he wished to delay it for as long as possible. Wanted to extend the exploration of Olivia.

She continued to work her hips along with his motions, and he didn't stop. Because she didn't ask him to. He simply watched her, watched and tried to match his rhythm to her own, to learn her. Because she was teaching him, with each breath, each sound, each gentle roll of her hips.

He slid his thumb back and forth over the bundle of nerves he'd been teasing and a gasp shook her body, her internal muscles pulsing around him, her entire being trembling.

He knew what that was. He had read about it.

And he had helped her achieve it.

Satisfaction that surely rivaled any orgasm broke over him.

At the same time his pride roared around inside him like a beast, a sense of overwhelming humility overtook him.

His hands, these hands that had endured so much pain and caused so much pain, had done that to her.

He was not worthy of the gift.

Her eyes opened again, a sleepy look in them now. "You didn't even kiss me."

He withdrew from her body, leaning over and pressing his mouth to hers. It was slow, exploratory, and he allowed her to lead now. She cupped his face, her soft hand resting on his cheek. She shifted, bringing her body into full contact with his.

She lifted her head, a half smile on her lips, and then she lowered her hand, pressing her palm to his hardened arousal. "I think it's your turn."

She curled her fingers around him through the fabric of his pants, heat cracking over him like a whip. And he couldn't pretend this was all about her anymore. These appetites had always seemed a weakness to him. A part of his brother's corruption; a part of man's corruption. And yet, he could feel no corruption here in this.

Not here in this room that had become their sanctuary. No one else was invited; no one else and nothing else could gain a foothold here. A storm could be raging outside and the two of them would never know, shielded here, buffeted by the thick walls of the palace. This concerned only the two of them, and for the first time he understood that corruption crept in when the door was left open. But with it closed now, barred, in their own private refuge, he felt he was gathering strength rather than losing it.

That in fact, this might be the safest place for him to lose control, so that he might better rebuild it when he was outside these walls.

He would put up no argument to that conclusion at all. He was incapable.

He looked down at her, at the gleam in her blue eyes.

Wicked, provocative. She squeezed him gently and a wave of desire moved through him.

He was a man after all. For surely stone could not feel these things. She sat up, getting onto her knees, leaning into him, increasing the pressure of her touch.

His throat tightened and he swallowed hard, his chest aching. Being stone, he imagined, was in many ways easier than being a man. But a stone could feel no excitement at the touch of Olivia's hand. And that meant he had no desire for the ease that might come with life as a rock.

She surprised him then, not going to the closure of his trousers, but to the buttons on his shirt. He stayed motionless while she set about her task. Removing his tie, pushing his jacket to the floor, followed by his shirt. And then her hands went to the closure of his pants. Her movements were deft, certain, as she divested him of the rest of his clothing.

When he was naked before her, she pressed her palm against him again, her breath hissing through her teeth. He had no idea what expectation females might have of the male body. And he had never had a reason to cultivate modesty. So he found himself now standing before her, not nervous, but assessing.

A small sound escaped her lips that was akin to a whimper.

"Tell me your thoughts," he commanded.

Perhaps this was not the best time to be talking, but he found that he needed to know what was on her mind. And he had no experience of reading people. Not like this.

"I'm impressed," she said, her voice thick, husky. She traced the ridge of his erection with the tip of her finger, her eyes never leaving his. "You are most impressive."

"Am I?"

She blinked. "Surely you know. I cannot be the only woman to praise your natural endowments."

"You are."

Her eyes widened. "Then, the other women you've been with have very bad manners."

"I have never been with a woman before." The admission broke past his lips and his best intentions to keep this a secret.

She jerked her hand back as though she'd been burned. "What?"

"I told you. I had taken a vow to cast off earthly pleasures. I had to keep my focus. I could not be allowed to be distracted, even for a moment."

"Somehow I didn't imagine you meant you had cast off everything."

"Is it so unusual?"

Something in her expression softened. "In my experience, that would be the last thing a man chose to discard."

"I can see that. My brother was consumed by his lusts. For power. For women. I thought it best not to taint myself with those needs."

"And now?"

"My responsibilities have changed. They now include you."

A crease formed between her brows. "I'm not sure if I like the idea of this being a responsibility."

He reached out and wrapped his fingers around her wrist, drawing her palm back to his arousal. "Does this feel like a responsibility?"

"No. It certainly doesn't."

"I want this," he said, barely able to force the words through his throat. "But I know very little about what I'm supposed to do to ensure your pleasure. I read a book."

"You read a book?"

"Yes. To better learn how to please you."

Color heightened in her cheeks. "Well, you've done a good job so far."

He took hold of her chin with his thumb and forefinger and tilted her face upward. "Have I? Have I pleased you?"

"Yes. You couldn't tell?"

"I felt you. I felt you climax around my fingers."

She blushed. Somehow he had made her blush. He found that near as heady a rush as making her climax had been. "You're a good study."

"I am a thorough man. In all things." He swallowed, looking down at her body. "And you are far too precious for me to approach this with no skill. With no control."

"I had no complaints about your skill."

"Perhaps I have been too honest."

"No." She pressed her hands against his chest, bracing herself against him. "I'm glad you were honest."

She looked up at him, then focused in on his torso, pressing a kiss there. He closed his eyes, doing his best to maintain his hold on his control. What control he had. Dimly, he thought back to his earlier realization that allowing her to have his control here, in this place, might make him stronger outside of it.

She angled her head, kissing him lower, and he reached back and grabbed hold of her hair, working his fingers through the soft blond strands. She wrapped her fingers tightly around the base of his shaft, squeezing him as she curved her lips around the head.

He tightened his grip on her, flexing his hips toward her. She widened her mouth, taking him in deeper. White light exploded behind his eyes and he gritted his teeth hard to keep himself from reaching his release then and there. He had never conceived of such pleasure. Never imagined the intensity that might come from wrapping something other than his own fist around his body. Certainly, there had been times when he hadn't been able to transcend the ache, that knot deep in his gut late at night. Then he had dealt with it quickly, as efficiently as possible. But this wasn't about efficiency. This wasn't about simply satisfying the ache. This was about relishing it. Enjoying every pass of her tongue along his length, every sweet jolt of pleasure wrapped up in pain.

He recalled then the pain he had experienced at the hand of his brother. Pain designed to break him.

He looked down at the soft, beautiful woman pleasuring him with her mouth, subjecting him to a new kind of torture. He was as out of control now as he had been then. At the mercy of his captor. But he had never had such a beautiful captor.

Her gentle hands on the most male part of him were more powerful than any whip brought across his skin had ever been. He had a feeling she could turn the tide inside him with a flick of her wrist. Or rather, a skilled turn of her tongue.

She took him in deeper, and he could think no more. There was nothing, nothing but a blessed blankness, carrying him through the darkness on a wave of sensation. He had, at points in his life, been filled so full of pain he had been afraid it would burst forth from him in an endless torrent. That it was too much for his physical being to contain. A knife plunging into his skin, deeper and deeper, until he was certain it would hit something vital and end him forever.

Now it felt as if the blade had turned. And it was still too much. Still too deep. But it was pleasure he was drowning in rather than pain.

He gritted his teeth, so near the edge he wasn't certain how long he could hold himself back from going over. But the idea of finishing like this horrified him. He couldn't subject her to that. Her lips were on him. Surely that was not acceptable. Even he with his limited experience knew that.

He tightened his hold on her hair, tugging her backward. "Enough," he said, "I cannot endure any more."

"Good," she said. "I want you inside me."

Her words made his stomach pitch. "I'm not sure I can withstand it." His voice was rough, his words honest.

"We can only try," she said. Smooth, perfect Olivia. As always. She never seemed ruffled. Never seemed at sea.

He felt certain that he must make it a goal to see her as lost and desperate as he was.

He growled, pressing her back into the mattress, gripping her wrists and holding them above her head. Much like the voluntary position she had assumed earlier. He parted her legs roughly with his own, settling between her thighs. "I will do more than try," he said.

He might be a virgin, but he was also a warrior. Was a man who led troops into battle. Toward death, and yet ensuring they never in fact met that darkest of demons.

Surely if he could march into a line of enemy soldiers, he could breach a woman's body.

He kissed her neck, because she looked delicious and he wanted to, and she arched against him, her breasts pressing firmly into his chest, her hips tilting upward. The head of his arousal met against her slick entrance. Yet again it was as though a blade had twisted inside him, a new brand of pleasure and pain bursting through him.

He wanted nothing more than to sink into her. The promise of all that heat, so sweet and slick, sheathing his body, pushed him to the brink.

"Say you want this," he ground out, his lips still pressed against her neck.

"Yes. Tarek. I want this. Please." She lifted her hips off the bed, pressing herself more firmly against him.

And he couldn't hold back any longer.

He pressed against the opening to her body and entered her slowly, gritting his teeth as she surrounded him. Inch by excruciating inch.

He trembled, burying his face in her neck as he tried

to hold back the orgasm that was threatening to end this before it even began.

He thought back to his long years in the desert. Barren, dry years that stretched before him as far as he could see. Blank, pale sand meeting a washed-out sky.

He thought of all the years he'd been without touch. Without anyone to speak to. Anyone to hold him.

He was here now. And so was she. And he would be damned to hell if he let it end now.

This was his due. For every slash in his skin made by a blade. For every lash of the whip. Every moment he'd gone without food or water. So much deprivation. And here he was submerged in sensation. In her.

Now, for the first time, he would maintain control, not for the sake of anyone else. But for himself. Only for himself.

He lifted his head, looked down at her. Her eyes were closed, her lips parted, cheeks flushed. He lifted his hand, traced her lower lip with his thumb. Could feel his body respond, pulsing deep inside hers.

He kissed her mouth, relishing her flavor, relishing the moment.

And then his control slipped its leash. He couldn't stay still any longer. He withdrew, before thrusting back in deep. Repeating the motion when she moaned, the sound spurring him on.

She wrapped her legs around his hips, arching against him, urging him on. She whispered in his ear. Pleas, cries. All in English. His brain lost the ability to translate, her words losing their meaning as he moved with her.

She met his every thrust, pressing hard against him when he was sheathed fully within her. She shook in his arms, coming apart completely, her internal muscles tightening down hard on him as she gave herself over to her release.

And then he let go. And he was falling over the edge.

Blood roared through his ears, howling like a beast as he lost himself in his climax. In her. Olivia.

He opened his eyes, cupped her face, met her gaze. Her eyes were wide, shocked. Until she closed them. Looked away.

"Olivia," he said, his voice rough. Unrecognizable.

She shifted beneath him, a small squeak escaping her lips. "Could I just…?"

"Sorry." He rolled to the side, allowing her space. She sat up, drawing her knees to her chest, and he stayed where he was. On his side, his head propped up by his hand.

He gazed at the lines, the curves of her body. He couldn't stop staring. She was beautiful. The most beautiful thing he had ever seen. Just looking at her was like water on parched earth. Healing. Reaching deep, untouched places inside him. Bringing them life.

She placed her hands on his arm, slowly letting her fingertips drift along his bare skin. "Tarek…you are so beautiful." She touched a scar on his arm. "So fierce. So caring. That was… I have no words for it. Why have you never been with anyone? Why do you deny yourself?" She took a shuddering breath. "Tarek, what did he do to you?"

CHAPTER TEN

HE SHOOK HIS HEAD. "We don't need to speak of it. Not now."

She nodded slowly, keeping her hand on his arm. She didn't speak for a moment, her eyes downcast. Then she looked back up at him. "You've really never been with a woman before?"

"No."

"Have you... What...what have you done with...other people...?"

"No one. Nothing. I cannot remember the last time I was touched at all before you." And suddenly the weight of her fingertips on his arm was like a brick. So heavy it was nearly unbearable.

"You were very good," she said. "You should know that."

Never in his memory had anyone said something to him out of interest of sparing his feelings. But he wondered now if that was the case. "There is no need for you to lie. In fact, it is best if you don't. I need to learn how to please you."

"You did. I'm not lying to you. Trust me, I wouldn't. I was not a... You know I was with my husband. He was the only one. But...I say that to tell you I understand how important communication is. Especially in the bedroom."

"I imagine he did not need instruction."

"No," she said, looking down. "He didn't. Though, in some ways, he did. Anytime you're with someone new you must learn them. All bodies are not the same. Being with you is different."

"And does it please you?"

"Yes," she said, meeting his eyes, leaving off any sarcastic asides.

"If I had known...if I had known what it would be like, I never could have resisted you the day that you touched me."

A smile curved her lips. "Really?"

"Yes, really. I am a terrible liar. If I suffer from anything, it might be too much honesty."

"I've noticed that. I find it quite refreshing."

"Why is that?"

The smile inverted, a slight crease appearing between her brows. "I'm not sure. Maybe because I have spent very much of my life around careful people. I've spent much of my life being careful and suffering consequences when I wasn't. I quite like that you aren't."

"I suppose carefulness might be a valuable skill to cultivate."

"If I teach you, you have to promise never to use it on me."

"An odd request."

"Maybe I'm odd." She tilted her head to the side, something about the motion making his heart feel slightly overlarge for his chest.

"I think of the two of us, I am the strange one."

"Possibly." She lay back on the bed, temptation personified. He could easily get lost in her. Make love to her until they both fell asleep.

And what will happen when sleep comes?

Ice replaced the blood flowing through his veins.

"It is time, I think, for you to go back to your room," he said.

"What? I just thought..."

"For many reasons, not the least of which being that I

have yet to solve the sleepwalking-with-weapons issue, I think it would be best if we kept to our separate quarters."

She nodded slowly. "I anticipated that we would have separate rooms in general, but I thought perhaps tonight…"

"There is the issue of the sword."

"Perhaps chuck it out into the hall?" she asked, one brow raised.

"I could, but then what else might I get hold of? I'm very resourceful."

She raised her other brow. "Are you? I feel as if I've just benefited from some of that resourcefulness."

That cool top layer of hers was back in place. It was because he'd hurt her in some way, and he could sense that. But he couldn't fathom what he might do to fix it. Not when her fingers on his arm were crushing him now. Not when he needed space. Not just from her, but beyond these walls. Out in the desert.

But failing that, he just needed to be alone. He needed time to process. Time to rebuild. He couldn't do that with her here.

"Please do not take this personally," he said. "Please don't be hurt."

She shook her head slowly, removing her touch from him. "It doesn't work that way, Tarek."

"Why not?" Not even he was that obtuse when it came to interacting with people. Still, it seemed unfair.

"You can't call a bullet back after it's been fired. I would think that's something a warrior would understand."

"But I didn't mean to fire at you."

She put her hand on his cheek. "You know that doesn't matter, either."

"It is for your safety."

She tilted her head to the side. "I'm sure it is. Good night, Tarek."

She slipped from his bed, taking her wedding gown

from the floor and slipping it back on, holding the front closed, not bothering to collect anything else. Not her bangles, not her veil, not her belt.

She had entered the chamber a bride, and she was leaving a wife. An unhappy wife.

But he had to set limits, even now. It was best she learned. When it came to sharing his body, he had determined to give. Because he could do nothing else, in truth. But there were other things that must remain off-limits.

He had whittled the focus of his soul down to a sleek, streamlined arrow, with all of the excess shaved away. He could not go back. He would not.

Yes, his body he could afford to share. But never his soul. He could never, ever expose her to everything he'd been through. Never share the creation of his scars.

She was far too lovely for him to ever present her with something so ugly.

Difficult, when the ugliness was written all over his body.

And one more reason to stay out of her bed tonight.

Olivia was playing petulant games, and she knew they would come to nothing with Tarek. Removing herself from her first husband's bed for a certain length of time when she'd found him irritating had typically resulted in the desired apology. Because Marcus didn't want to be without sex, he would say whatever he needed to in order to restore harmony in that area. Tarek, of course, wouldn't understand. She was attempting to manipulate a man who was impossible to manipulate. Not because he was so strong, but because he simply didn't understand subterfuge.

She felt wretched.

But he had torn her open on their wedding night, laid her bare in more ways than just the physical. The way he had looked at her... As though she was special, as though she was the only one. Her heart seized tight. It was because she was the only one. The only woman to ever touch him. The only woman to ever kiss him, to have him inside her body.

It forced more unfavorable comparisons between him and her first husband.

Marcus had been skilled. He had been with countless women before she'd come into his life. For him seduction had been about knowing exactly where to touch, exactly how.

He'd left her feeling as if she was floating on a cloud, left her feeling sated and satisfied.

Tarek had left her bruised. Aching. Desperate for more.

There was something so impolite about the way he had ravished her. Like the man himself. In contrast, Marcus had unfailing manners, always. But Olivia couldn't escape the thought that it was a testament to how little it mattered which female was in his bed at any given time.

She had spoken to Tarek about how they would both have to learn. Of course she would have to take the time to watch his responses, to feel what made him shake. What made him moan. What made him hard. But then she'd realized that hadn't been the case with Marcus. He had never *learned* her in that way. He knew women. That was different.

Not that she had cause for complaint; not that she never asked for more.

It was pointless to stand here and compare two men who were completely different. Particularly when one was dead, couldn't give more even if she begged him to. And she hadn't. When he'd been alive she'd asked him for nothing beyond what he gave.

Unlike Tarek, Marcus had never pledged fidelity.

She'd never asked him to.

You didn't ask Tarek to, either.

And yet he had.

None of this made her wonder what was wrong with Marcus. Rather, she was beginning to wonder what was wrong with herself. Why she had never pushed for more. Because she and Marcus had professed love for each other, and still he had given her less than half. And she had accepted it. Not only had she accepted it, she'd been comfortable with it. Had he made eye contact with her as he thrust deep into her body the way that Tarek had, she probably would have curled in on herself and retreated.

Intimacy meant reaching deep. It meant sharing and changing. Turning over things that were wrong and discovering how they could be fixed. Facing problems head-on.

That had never gone well for her in the past. The potential cost felt too great.

For that reason, she hadn't wanted that sort of intimacy with the man she'd once called her husband.

She wasn't entirely certain she wanted it now. Because that intimacy was the reason she was avoiding Tarek's bed in a fit of pique. His rough, unpracticed movements, that it was all for her, only for her, had stripped a layer of skin from her body, left her raw and exposed. And then, after all that, he had asked her to leave. When she had wanted nothing more than to wrap her arms around his waist and curl up beside him, bury her face in the curve of his neck. Lie with him until her breathing matched his, until they both drifted off to sleep.

He had denied her that.

She was still angry. Still angry, even knowing she had to get into a limousine with him and go down into the capital city for him to make a speech at a monument of war to commemorate a day in the nation's history. It was, in her understanding, a celebration of the founding of the country. The unification of the primary tribes into one sovereign nation. And of course Tarek would need to be there, again speaking of unity, and of the new future for Tahar.

And she, as the new sheikha, had to accompany him and stand just behind him, staring at him adoringly while she really wanted to eviscerate him. Possibly with her teeth. All right, she was being both dramatic and bloodthirsty.

She walked through the throne room of the palace to the antechamber that led outside. She paused, adjusting the scarf she had wound over her hair and loosely around her neck. Then she walked outside, putting on a pair of large sunglasses to protect her from the glare, and from Tarek's gaze.

He was already standing there, in front of the limousine. He was wearing a dark suit jacket and perfectly cut trousers, his hands stuffed into the pockets. His shoulders were broad, his waist narrow, and not even the superbly cut pants could disguise the perfection that was the musculature of his thighs. She thought it was funny how quickly he had taken to wearing European-style suits. He seemed to like them. Or perhaps he simply didn't want to bother to have anything else tailored. That could be it. Nothing off the rack was going to fit him. He was too tall, too broad.

She was obsessed with his body. Which wouldn't be so much of an issue if she wasn't also obsessed with the man. A man who was nearly impossible to reach.

"Good morning," she said, opting for the first thrust so that it was his job to parry.

He turned and her stomach lurched. She chose to imagine him still as the great hairy beast-man she had initially encountered in the throne room. But considering that, she sometimes forgot just how beautiful he was. It was easy to focus only on the raw magnetism and forget that he was objectively the most handsome man she had ever seen.

"You are speaking to me, Olivia," he said, his eyes flicking over her.

She wondered if she should have worn a dress. Or perhaps something more traditionally Tahari. She thought perhaps her cream-colored harem pants, gold blouse tucked into the high waist and long, loose linen jacket might not be the appropriate attire. If he noticed, he didn't say.

"You do not have to cover your hair," he said, jerking open the door to the limousine.

"I know. Wind." She breezed past him and got into the car, sliding to the other side and buckling herself with a resolute click.

And Tarek insulation, but he didn't need to know that. For that same reason, she kept her sunglasses in place.

"We will be staying in the city tonight," he said, joining her in the limo, closing the door behind him.

The car began to move away from the palace as she processed this piece of information.

"I didn't bring anything."

"It was taken care of for you."

Of course it was.

"You are angry with me," he continued. "You haven't spoken to me in two days."

"Very good, Tarek. Next we'll move on to the more advanced human emotions."

"I explained to you why I didn't want you in my room."

"I don't believe you," she bit out. Her words lingered in the air, bitter, desperate to her ears.

"You want to stay with me?"

"Yes. I do."

The admission was difficult, which she despised. Exposing all of her neediness, all of the desire in her that had gone unmet for so many years. Because of herself. Because she had never asked for more. Because she had been terrified of more. She still was. But she also felt as if she had been breathing stale air for too long, and Tarek was like the very wind she'd claimed to be trying to protect her hair from. A rush of something fresh, necessary, that she could not control or harness. But it wasn't her hair she was concerned for.

It was her heart. That caged, protected creature that she had locked behind golden bars years ago. Because she had been so tired of feeling the hurt every time her parents missed something special of hers because they needed to be with Emily. Because what kind of monster did it make her if she wanted the attention stolen from her sick sister and directed at her? It was why she had been able to accept Marcus's love for what it was. Why she had been able to love him in return while knowing almost nothing about him, and sharing almost nothing about herself.

She didn't like any of these revelations. Not in the least. Any more than she liked the revelation that Tarek had disrespected the cage. Had stuck his hands right between the bars and grabbed hold of the thing she'd been coddling the most.

Bastard.

He didn't even know. Hadn't even been aiming for her affected organ, she knew. She supposed that was the danger of sleeping with virgins. They were so honest. And everything they gave was all for you.

As a woman who had never had anything that was just for her, she'd been unprepared for what it would do to her.

Marrying a stranger, a feral stranger, who lived across the world, who had completely different customs and practices than she did, surely should have been a recipe for continuing on in the manner she had become accustomed to. Surely he was the last person on earth who should have ever been able to reach her.

She was wretched indeed. And irritated that she was having these realizations while sitting next to him in a car. It wasn't as if she could jump out of the moving vehicle to escape him.

On second thought, at the moment it sounded preferable to continuing to be enclosed in this tiny space with him.

Alas, she wasn't going to take a chance on a tuck and roll at this moment.

Which meant she simply had to endure.

The limousine wound down a narrow street that widened into a highway, leading them from the outskirts of the city down into its heart. It was much more urban than Alansund, and while she had known that, seeing it was an entirely different matter. Living with Tarek as she did, in a palace that was a relic from another time, it was easy to forget that the country itself was a major world power. A capital of finance and technology.

They moved down deeper into the central business district, the buildings rising around them like sharp, slate-gray waves, threatening to close in on them. She had been raised in New York, upstate, but also partly in Manhattan. She was accustomed to cities. And yet, right now this felt a more foreign landscape than the barren desert that provided her view out her bedchamber at the palace.

It was strange how quickly that place had become her home. Her world.

Strange how quickly Tarek had managed to weave himself around her existence.

The entire car ride was silent. Filled with tension, her head filling with things she would never speak. Finally, they arrived at the memorial statue of a man riding a horse, symbolizing the nation's strength. This was where his speech would be held. Already a crowd had assembled, and security detail was on hand.

The bodyguards approached the car, opening the doors for them and flanking them both as they made their way to the podium that was prepared for Tarek's speech. She removed her sunglasses as they walked to the front, taking her position at his right shoulder, a pace behind him.

She knew this pose. The pose of any royal spouse or politician's wife. She had assumed it many times for Marcus.

But it had felt different.

Because now, watching Tarek speak, words she didn't readily understand due to her poor command of the language, she felt a burst of pride unlike anything she ever experienced before. This wasn't easy for him. This was not his forte. He was a man who had barely spoken to people for the past fifteen years, much less spoken in front of a crowd of them. And yet he was doing it. Because he loved this country, because he cared for it.

He was changing everything about his life, everything about himself, to become the leader that Tahar needed.

Life was always a challenge, even when you were doing all that you had been created for. All that you had been made for.

But how much more challenging must it be to perform tasks you had never imagined being asked to do?

She watched his every dynamic action until he was finished, until thunderous applause filled the air around them. And then, only then, did she look at the faces of those in the crowd. And she saw their hope. Saw their admiration.

Her heart fluttered against its cage.

After that, she was caught up again in the rush of security detail, ushering them back to the limousine. When they were safely inside, Tarek let out a breath she imagined he had been holding for the past twenty minutes.

"You did well," she said, forgetting her annoyance for a moment.

"Now we must go to a hotel a few blocks downtown. It has something to do with tradition. Some sort of honor for the owner. It is the oldest hotel of its kind in the city. Of course, it has been greatly modernized, I have been assured. Not that I much mind if something isn't modern. I'm used to caves after all."

"I'm sure they'll appreciate it." She looked down. "Did you secure us separate rooms? Or did you give consideration to the gossip that might stir up?" she asked, breaking their momentary truce.

"We have been given the penthouse suite. I imagine that will give us adequate space."

"I don't know. I hear you're very resourceful. Or did you pack your sword?"

"Do not test me, Olivia. I am aware that I have given you the impression that I'm some sort of house cat. Because you have caught me attempting to become domesticated. But I assure you, I am more tiger than tabby. Do not make me demonstrate it."

"You show rather more restraint than a tiger. You allowed me to spend two days ignoring you, and you never once challenged me."

She suddenly found herself pressed against the door, Tarek's hands on either side of her, his body against hers. "Do not think you can manipulate me. You have seen me at a disadvantage, acclimating to a position that I was not created for. But I am not to be toyed with. I am not to be teased. I am not your aristocratic husband. Never forget you cannot play the same games with me."

"No worries. I am in no danger of forgetting that you aren't Marcus." She would let him believe whatever he wanted to about that statement.

"See that you don't," he bit out.

The limousine pulled up to the front of the grand stone building. It reminded her more of places she had seen in Europe than she had expected it to.

"A holdover from our brush with colonialism, I believe," he said.

"I wondered," she said, because she had. And architecture was a welcome subject change. Really, anything was a welcome subject change at this point. Her irritation with him was betraying too much, not only to him, but to herself. She didn't want to analyze her feelings as deeply as her anger was commanding.

Tarek didn't wait for their driver. He opened the door to the vehicle, rounding the back of it and holding hers open, as well. She exited, and he looped his arm around hers, taking hold of her and leading her into the building.

There was little evidence of modernization in the lobby. Golden revolving doors led into a grand marble showcase. Crystal chandeliers hung from the domed ceiling, curved staircases flanking either side of the room.

Every member of staff in the room stood at attention, but none approached. It was the owner who made his way through the center of the room, approaching them with a wide smile on his face and his hand outstretched. Tarek shook it, and Olivia did the same.

"Welcome, Sheikh Tarek. Sheikha." He swept his hand wide, indicating their surroundings. "We are most pleased you have joined us. As you may know, this hotel has housed every member of the royal family since it was built. We have readied our finest room. This is doubly special, as we are not only celebrating a new leader, but a new marriage."

"Thank you," Olivia said, certain she didn't sound very convincing at all.

"The suite is on the top floor," the man continued, handing Tarek a key card. "Would you like us to show you there, or will you make your own way?"

"I think we can make our own way," Tarek said. She wondered if playing at civility was starting to chafe.

She knew it was for her. She couldn't stand there smiling at him as though their interaction in the car hadn't happened. As though the past few days hadn't happened.

"We will have your luggage sent up directly, after you've had a moment to settle in."

"Appreciated," Tarek said.

He sounded less than appreciative. But at least he had tried. She was just standing beside him, silent, still. She may as well have been a pillar of salt. But she was a pillar of salt who could walk. She followed Tarek to the elevator bank and stepped into the lift with him, her breath freezing in her chest as the doors slid closed behind them. Here she was again, back in an enclosed space with the man who was driving her crazy.

This was ridiculous. She didn't get crazy over men. She didn't get crazy over anything.

Except Tarek. She had already admitted that everything about him was different. That he was reaching places she'd thought unreachable. There was no point playing as if she was confused now.

They completed the elevator ride in silence, and Olivia wondered what had happened to all of her social graces. She'd had them at one point, she was certain. In another life she had been a queen, confident both in her position, and in how to deal with her marriage.

Because you wanted nothing from it. But you need to matter to him. And you want to understand him.

She blew out a harsh breath, singularly frustrated with herself. She didn't want deep personal insight. Not now, possibly not ever. But then, reflecting on the past wasn't really very helpful, either. Particularly, because when she thought of the past, she felt as though she was pondering a different woman. She barely recognized that woman. In many ways, she barely recognized the woman she'd been when she'd walked into the throne room to tell Tarek she thought they should marry.

Because her reasons had been different then. They had had nothing to do with Tarek and everything to do with herself. With her desperation to find a place in life. To keep herself surrounded by enough things, enough people to feel as if she wasn't alone. To cover up the yawning pit of need that was in the center of her chest.

Suddenly, Tarek mattered. Suddenly, it wasn't just about not being alone. Though she was tired of that, too. Because she realized that she'd been alone for a very long time. Even when surrounded by people. Even when sleeping next to the first man she had married.

She watched her current husband, the only one who *mattered*, walk out of the elevator and up to the only door in the narrow hallway. He used the key card in the lock, the light turning green instantly.

"You know how to use one of those?"

He raised a brow. "It's fairly self-explanatory."

"Well, I'm having a hard time figuring out what is self-explanatory for you and what isn't. The female body, obviously, was fairly self-explanatory. Female feelings, on the other hand…"

He held up the key card, the strip facing her. "I dare say this is a much more simple device than your inner workings. Also, if I could swipe this across your forehead and gain access to your secrets, I would."

"Are you saying women are complicated?"

"I am simply saying I do wonder sometimes if life is better lived alone. And if sex is perhaps not worth the trouble it causes."

"One time and you're an expert in the consequences of sex?"

"I am living them," he said, his tone telegraphing his foul mood. Well, she was just as foul. Fouler even.

"If it was just sex it wouldn't be a problem."

"Is it not just sex?"

She shook her head. "No. Don't you know that?"

"How would I know? I don't know what *only sex* is supposed to feel like." He pushed the door open and revealed an opulent suite, beautifully appointed.

It was indeed the epitome of modern luxury. But as she had spent most of her life steeped in modern luxury, there was a limit to how impressed she could be. Particularly when she had other matters on her mind.

"Are you supposed to feel as though your internal organs were ripped out through your chest and displayed for all the world? Are you supposed to feel like you can't breathe whenever you remember what it was to be skin to skin with another person? Are you supposed to ache down to your very bones? If so, then I suppose I have an all right understanding of what it means to engage in sex."

"No," she said, her chest so tight she could barely breathe. "*Just sex* makes you feel good. I don't even know what *this* is."

"You will see that I am delighted to be unique to you, my queen." He sounded nothing close to delighted at all.

"Oh, you could never be anything but, my sheikh," she said, taking a step closer to him. "I have never experienced anything remotely similar to you."

"For a start," he said, his tone brittle, "I do not know how to smile."

She took another step toward him. "Not well."

He gripped her chin between his thumb and forefinger and held her fast, dipping his head suddenly and kissing her, hard, deep. The kiss bruised, wounded. And she didn't mind. Because it reflected what was going on inside her. And then, just as abruptly as he descended, he pulled away. "I need a shower," he said, turning and walking from the room.

He left her standing there, feeling dizzy. Angry. What was happening to her? Why was this man…this…*virgin*… causing her so much trouble? She had been married to a man whose skills as a lover were world renowned. Why was she so much more affected, why was she destroyed, wrecked, by a man who had never even kissed a woman before her? Her heart twisted tight. That was why. That was why she was so affected. She was unique to him. She made him feel. She reached him.

Had she ever been special to anyone else in her entire life? Had she ever been special to her parents? Had she ever been special to her husband?

Had she ever been special to herself? Or had she simply been so afraid she'd set about to make herself whatever she needed to be in order to keep from feeling lonely? Keep from feeling exposed? Had she ever mattered enough to her own self to demand a thing?

Not beyond that one failure.

Because in that moment, when she'd shouted her parents down for missing the party she'd thrown for herself, she had to face the fear that she wasn't worthy of all she craved.

Face it. Live it. Accept it.

But it didn't stop her from needing. And she'd been so sure that her neediness was wrong, shameful, because no one would ever want to meet it.

But now she was tired of it. So tired of feeling as if she was living behind a wall, with the walls of everyone around her standing between both of them. She was tired. Tired and alone, and she hated it. She wanted to be touched. She wanted to touch someone in return. She didn't want nice; she didn't want pleasant. She wanted real.

She stripped her jacket off, letting it fall to the floor, followed by her gold top, and her pants. As she made her way into the bathroom she rid herself of her undergarments, opened the door, stopping when she saw the broad expanse of Tarek's naked back. He was standing beneath the hot spray, water droplets rolling down his skin.

And she was transfixed. Not just by the beautiful musculature she saw there, not just by his bronzed skin and the perfection of his butt.

It was the scars.

She had examined the front of him, his chest, his abs. Had touched him there. But she realized now she had never really looked at his back. He had been whipped. More than that, tortured. And it was written across that beautiful flesh, as bold as any pen stroke.

Olivia had never hated before. She did right now. Right now, she hated the man who would have been her brother-in-law. Hated him with a scorching fire that would never be satisfied.

He had done this. She knew he had.

She would kill him herself were he not already dead, and not lose any sleep over it.

She said nothing, approaching the shower and opening the solid glass door, stepping inside behind him, wrapping her arms around his waist and resting her head against his scarred body. "I'm sorry."

She didn't know if she was apologizing for the words they had exchanged outside or for the atrocities he had endured. Possibly both. Possibly for everything, even things she didn't know about yet. Things she hadn't done yet.

He was unique, this man. So special. And she had been petty. Of course he didn't respond to things in any way she could anticipate. He was an entirely new creature to her. There was no past experience to call on to help her here.

He stiffened beneath her touch. But he didn't pull away, and nor did he turn.

"I am very likely the one who should be sorry," he said. "I don't know what to do with you."

"If you are lost, I don't know what hope the rest of us have."

She smoothed her hands over his chest, the water making his skin slick. "What does that mean?"

"You always know what to do, Olivia."

"Not right now. Right now, I'm just as lost as you are."

He shifted then, turning and backing her against the

wall, his erection hard against her hip, his dark gaze intense on hers. "I know what I want."

"What?" she asked, her voice thin.

"You."

"Have me."

On a growl, he lowered his head, kissing her, harder than he had done out in the living area. This wasn't a kiss filled with anger, but of desperation. Desperation that reflected her own. She smoothed her hands down over his back, the scar tissue beneath her hands obvious now. She had missed it the first night they'd made love. She'd had her hands on his shoulders as he'd thrust deep inside her, but she hadn't realized what it meant. She did now. And she ached, not just with the need for him, but the need to heal him. The need to reach him. If she had to crack herself open wide, show him by example, she would. She would.

She reached down, grabbing hold of his thick arousal, shifting their positions and widening her stance, placing ahead of him the slick entrance to her body. "Please," she whispered.

He flexed his hips, finding her center unerringly, moving deep within her.

Hot water rolled over them, his kisses raining down on her face to match each drop. Tarek was inside her. And she wasn't alone. Wasn't separate from him. She opened her eyes, meeting his dark, raw gaze. He saw her. She was not just a body, not simply a pleasant diversion, or a duty. He needed this; he needed her.

And she needed him. For the first time in her life, that idea didn't terrify her to her core. She needed him, and it made her feel wonderful. Made her feel beautiful. Made her feel strong.

Because if she didn't give up herself, Tarek would never be able to release the walls that surrounded his own heart. She knew it then, as sure she knew anything else.

She moved her hands down, grabbing hold of his be-hind, tugging him hard against her, gasping as her orgasm washed over her, the pleasure blinding, like nothing else she had ever experienced. She didn't hold back the cries on her lips, didn't hold back anything. She poured herself, all of herself, into it. And when he found his own release, she gloried in it. In the way he trembled, in the way he held her, his big hands braced against her hips, holding her steady as he rode the wave that threatened to consume them both.

Afterward there was no sound except for the water hitting the tile, their breath echoing in the small space.

"Let's go to bed," she said, her voice soft, firm. "Together."

He let out a ragged breath, kissed her neck. "For a while," he said, his tone cautious.

He turned the water off, and they got out of the shower. She took a crisp, folded white towel and began to drag it over his skin, erasing the water drops that covered his body. And he stood, allowing her to do it. As she did, she explored the scars that covered him. Memorized them. She felt honored to witness them. To feel them. Part of her wanted to close her eyes, to look away, to pretend she hadn't seen them.

But that was wrong. Someone had to see this. Someone had to care.

And she had to stop being so afraid to care.

Because she could no longer pretend that caring meant never asking questions, never asking anything of each other. That was benign neglect at best, masquerading as love simply because there was undemanding sex thrown into the mix.

A sharp pain worked its way through her, starting in her temples and spreading down, the ache blooming in her throat, then hitting hard in her chest. She had loved Marcus. She couldn't deny that. Not when the loss of him had thrown her into months of darkness, serious anxiety that had been difficult to shake. A feeling of loss and hopelessness that had been very real.

But she doubted in this moment if she had ever been in love with him. Their relationship hadn't allowed for feelings that cut half so deep. They had been partners, lovers, but it had been nothing like this. Tarek's pain lived inside her. Her triumph felt bound to his.

Do you still think of yourself as with him?

She flashed back to that question he'd asked her weeks ago during the coronation party. The answer had been simple. And it had been no. Because she had not been a part of Marcus.

Tarek was a part of her. Whether she was that for him or not, he was for her.

If she lost him, she knew very well that it would be like having her heart wrenched from her chest. It would be much harder to go on living. And that was the cost of love.

She loved him.

She wished, very much, in that moment, that she did not.

He took another towel from the counter and made it his mission to dry her. And by the time he was finished, by the time he scooped her up in his arms and carried her back into the bedroom, placed her gently on the bed, she knew that whether she wished it away or not, it was true. There had been no protecting herself from this. Nor from the pain that it could potentially bring.

Her desire to breach his defenses had caused her to lower her own.

She lay down on the bed, completely naked, unashamed, watching as he lay down beside her.

"Tell me about your back," she said, her voice hushed. Because she wanted the hard things. Because she wanted everything. Even if it was hard; even if it hurt. Even if it made her vulnerable.

"I told you. He tortured me."

"Why?" she asked, knowing she sounded broken, devastated. Perhaps that wasn't fair, when he spoke of it so calmly, but someone had to weep for him. It would be easy for her to do so.

"He said…he said the death of my parents was caused by weakness in the nation. He said I would have to be made strong. He said he did it because he loved Tahar. Because he loved me. He said it was the only way to protect the both of us."

"What did he…?"

He reached out and touched her breast, his thumb gentle as it slid over her nipple. "You are so soft, Olivia. So beautiful. I do not want to fill your head with the things that were done to me. There is only darkness and ugliness there. Nothing more."

"Don't hide from me. Please. I don't want that. I'm tired of pretending that someone lying next to me means I'm not alone. Especially when I realize that it isn't true."

"I don't understand. If you're lying next to someone, clearly you aren't alone."

"No. Trust me. Someone can lie next to you and still be miles away."

"Marcus?"

"This is our bed," she said, "I mean, this isn't our bed, it's the hotel's. But you know what I mean. I don't wish for him to be between us."

"I understand. But is that what you're talking about? Answer my question just this once."

"Yes. Him. But don't blame him. I never asked for more. And he never offered. I think he was protecting himself, as I was."

"There is certainly wisdom in protecting yourself."

Yes, but she was starting to see that she had been keeping herself wounded. Protecting herself from a fatal injury in her mind, but never fully healing the ones she'd already sustained.

"It's much better to protect other people, don't you think? You've certainly spent enough of your life doing that."

"With a sword. It's easy to protect yourself while you do that."

"I suppose it would be." She moved her fingertips over his arm, glorying in the feel of his bare skin beneath hers. "My parents didn't come to my fifteenth birthday. It's such a small thing compared to this." She brushed her palm over a raised scar on his arm, continuing, "But it hurt me. Scarred me. Scars you can't see. Our housekeepers made my birthday cakes. At least I had them. You didn't, I know."

"Olivia," he said, his voice rough. "My pain does not erase yours. Do not make what is so large for you smaller just because I, too, have suffered."

She swallowed hard. "You are...a wise man."

"I've spent a lot of time alone. I've had a lot of time to think."

"So you have." She hesitated. "For my fifteenth birthday I made my own cake. My own dinner. I told my family it would be special. I knew...I knew Emily couldn't come. She'd been in the hospital for a week. Her platelets were low and...anyway, I just asked my parents to come home for dinner. For my party." She blinked against a dry, painful stinging in her eyes. "They didn't come." The words were a whisper. "I waited and waited. They didn't come." She could feel his muscles tense beneath her touch. "I threw the cake away. I couldn't bear to eat it."

"Olivia..." His voice was rough.

"There's more. They got home late. And I...I yelled at

them. Why couldn't they spare a couple of hours for me? All I wanted was for them to spend more time at home with me. And my father just looked at me. My mother cried. Then he said…he said it wasn't like they wanted to be away. They didn't want to be in the hospital with a dying child. And how dare I want to take any time from Emily when she might die and…I was living. I shouldn't complain. Everything with them changed after that. It was never the same. Never."

"And so you left," he said. "Changed countries."

"Met a man I didn't want anything from. That helped. He didn't hurt me because…because I knew then never to demand anything. Never to make waves."

"Your parents were fools," he said.

"No. They were just in an impossible situation. They are."

"Perhaps you feel the need to be fair. I do not. They hurt you. That, in my mind, is all that matters. I judge them by that sin."

She took in a sharp, jagged breath, her fingertips trailing over his scarred flesh. "And I will judge Malik by his sins against you."

"He had me starved." Tarek rolled onto his back, his eyes focused on the ceiling. "He withheld water from me. To make me stronger," he said, his voice rough. "Because I would need to spend much time out in the desert, and there I would not always have food or drink. I had to be prepared. He had me beaten. Because I needed to learn strength. He whipped me. And he…" Tarek touched a patch on his arm that was smooth, shinier than the rest of his skin. "He liked fruit. I remember watching him peel the skin from a pear. He was perfectly capable of peeling off a layer of human skin with as much efficiency. I wear the evidence of that."

"Tarek. No," she said, her stomach twisting painfully.

"When I returned to the palace it all came back to me. That is why I woke from my sleep. That's why I walked the halls with a sword. To kill his ghost if he lingered. I could feel everything he'd done to me again. As though he was wounding me afresh. I found his journals. He admitted to having my parents assassinated. He...detailed the *work* he did on me to make me a loyal soldier. He liked the whips, as you saw. Liked to isolate me, as well. Deprive me of all sensory input, then...flay my skin with something sharp. My brother. My own brother. My parents were dead, and then...and then he betrayed me, and I have truly...truly never felt so alone as I did in that first moment when he tied me down and traced shapes in my back with the blade of his knife. That was when I started thinking of myself as a rock. Because a rock is unmoved. It might be reshaped, but it doesn't bleed. It will not die. It is simply reformed. And it remains strong. A rock is never weakened."

Olivia closed her eyes, stifling the sob that was climbing her throat. "How could he have done that to you? How?" They were empty words. Meaningless. And yet they were all she had.

"This is why I turn away from indulgences. From lusts of all kinds because...look at where it brought him."

"You aren't Malik."

"No," Tarek said, his voice blazing. "I know he did not intend it, but he gave me purpose. He ensured with all he did that I would guard myself against the weakness that infected his blood."

"Why? Why did he do it?"

"To break me, though he didn't say it. Strength, he said. It was always strength. Truly, I think he wanted me to rejoice in being banished to the desert. To make me hate the palace so much that I would never want to return. He wanted me too broken to rule. Too broken to realize his true character. Brainwashed. He did a magnificent job. Out there, I felt nothing. I had but one purpose—to fulfill the bargain I had made with my brother. The one that meant he would leave me be. There was clarity there. A beauty in the simplicity. I cherished it. In that way, I suppose he did his job. He made me strong. He made me the rock. He made that existence feel easy."

"It was a mind game. He didn't care for you. He didn't make you strong. You *were* strong. Any other man would have been broken."

He looked up at her, his eyes so black, so empty, they wounded her. "Was I not broken, Olivia?"

"No, Tarek. No. You are not broken." Her throat tightened, tears rolling down her cheeks. She put her hand on his chest, felt his heartbeat rage beneath her fingertips.

"Do not cry for me, Olivia. Not for me."

"Who else will?"

"No one needs to."

"That isn't true. It isn't."

"Whatever I was before Malik… Whatever happened before… I am different now. I'm another man. Whether or not I'm broken is immaterial. I am not what I should be. I can never be."

"You are everything you choose to be, Tarek," she said, the words ringing with conviction. "He cannot command control over you, not anymore."

"You don't understand. You don't understand the years I spent there. That they were my refuge. You cannot possibly understand what they meant to me, what they did to me."

"Make me understand. I'm tired of being alone, Tarek. I'm so tired of being alone. Let me see. Let me see you."

He rolled out of the bed, standing upright, naked, beautiful and unashamed. "Tomorrow," he said, his voice strained. "Tomorrow I will show you. I will make you understand. I am not the man you wish I could be. I am not the man you should have."

"But you have me," she said, as close to an admission as she could muster right now.

Pain flashed through his eyes, but almost as quickly as it appeared, it was replaced by the flatness again. "Tomorrow, I will show you."

"Tarek…" She blinked rapidly, looking down at her left hand, at the blue stone there. "Just…before you go… Why did you choose this ring for me?"

He looked at her, a subtle shift in his face softening his features. "Your eyes," he said. "The stone was blue. Like your eyes. And I very much liked the look of it. Since it made me think of you."

Her breath caught in her throat. A simple answer. But from Tarek…it may as well have been poetry. It was the truth. So simple. So perfect. It came from his soul, and touched her all the way down to hers.

Then he turned and walked out of the room, leaving her alone once again.

But this time, she didn't feel devastated by the loneliness. Because she wasn't simply going to lie back and allow it to be her fate. He had chosen this ring. Because of her eyes. That mattered. Because of that, she would fight.

It didn't matter what had happened before. Her fear had no place. Tarek was brave. A warrior to his soul. She would be nothing less for him. For herself.

With him, she would fight for more. With him, she would fight for everything.

CHAPTER ELEVEN

TAREK COULDN'T QUITE describe the feeling that took hold of him as they drove farther away from the city and deeper into the desert. It had surprised Olivia to know that he could drive a car. He supposed he couldn't blame her. There were a great many gaps in his education when it came to modern civilization. And while it was a skill he had not often used, it was one he possessed.

Thankfully all of his duties today had been office work, and he had managed to reschedule to make this time for Olivia.

He had demanded they go alone. He was more dangerous than any of the men on his security detail and had likely insulted them by saying so.

But this had been a necessity.

A dark, gnawing sense of panic had been chewing at him since yesterday. Possibly since their wedding night. Or perhaps even before that. Whenever it had appeared, it was only growing worse as they drove into the bleached, bone-dry wilderness.

It was as though the air in his lungs had been replaced with dust. Like drowning on land. He wondered why he was doing this. What he hoped to find out here. What he hoped to show her.

Last night she had looked at him with need and expectation. No one had ever looked at him like that before. Much less such a soft, vulnerable creature. And he had realized in that moment that being prepared to ride out into battle for her was not enough.

He knew nothing else. He knew nothing beyond living by the sword. He had heard somewhere that meant he would surely die by it, and if that was the case, he was prepared. He would die for her. He had no question on that score. But he had no idea what stood in between indifference and a willingness to sacrifice himself. It was those feelings, those things that frightened him.

Because they weren't a goal. They weren't an end point. It wasn't something clean and easy he could focus on.

The very idea splintered in his mind, confused him. Frightened him.

He could've laughed. Death didn't frighten him, but whatever the small, pale woman made him feel was the closest thing to terror he had experienced in his memory.

"How much farther?" she asked when they had been driving for well over two hours.

"Close now," he said. "There will be no one for miles. This time of year."

"What about other times of year?"

"There is a Bedouin tribe who pass this way routinely twice yearly. Often they would come to my settlement, for lack of a better word, and stay with me for a few days. I have also at times traveled with them. Though not often."

The shimmering horizon parted, and suddenly he could see the outlines of the skeletal buildings he had called home for fifteen years. He realized now why he had brought her here. To show her who he was. She had said she was tired of being alone, that she wanted to be with someone. Sadly for her, he was all she had. And this was all he was. She needed to see that; she needed to know.

He said nothing as his encampment drew nearer, and neither did she. It was as though a sandstorm had descended over them both, blanketing them completely, separating them sharply.

When he stopped the car, she remained silent. He killed the engine, opening the driver's-side door slowly, cautiously. He hadn't told her, but he was carrying a gun. He trusted nothing and no one. Anyone could have moved into this place in his absence.

"What exactly is this? Besides where you used to live," she said finally, coming to join him out there in the sand.

"It was a village. Much like the hotel, a part of Tahar's brush with colonialism. Two hundred years ago European settlers lived here. They didn't last." He looked around at the hollow stone buildings. "The houses did."

"Which one was yours?"

"They were all mine," he said.

"No. They weren't. Which one did you stay in?" she said, her persistence, and her insight, more disturbing than he would like to admit.

He took her hand in his and walked her through the settlement. He was prepared to reach for his weapon if need be, but he had no sense that anyone else was in residence.

He hadn't been back here since he had gotten word of his brother's death. It had been only a few months, and yet it felt like another lifetime.

They walked through the doorway, the two of them leaving footprints in the smooth sand. He looked down, at the smaller set next to his own. It was strange, to have her here with him. To see evidence that he wasn't alone.

Sand had washed through here like a flood, creeping up the sweeping staircase that was in the entryway of the two-story building. It was barren, empty, marred by years of wind, sun streaking through the unprotected windows and sandstorms.

It was bare, basic, and it was what he had known as home for half his life. He felt no relief, as he had imagined he might in his early days back at the palace. At first, he had imagined that going back to the simpler existence would be easier. But now he worried for his country. For the new position he had assumed. Now he realized he couldn't come out and get lost in the desert. Because there were those at the heart of the country who were now depending on him.

"This is where you lived?" Olivia asked, a note of horror winding through her voice.

"Yes," he said. "This is…this is my home."

"How did you survive this? How did you ever survive this?"

He didn't know how to answer that question. Because it hadn't been difficult. Surviving what had come before it…that had been the hard part. To live in this, he had become this. Barren. Empty. Void of anything but the basics. But the need to survive.

"This…this is a part of me. This is what I am." He indicated the empty, dry room. "This is all I am. I have purpose. But I am not…I am not more. Not more than this. I am not the beautiful, lavish halls of the palace. This is my soul. This is what's left."

"I don't believe that. I don't believe it, Tarek. You are more than this. You are more than what you were made."

"I am exactly what I was made," he said, his voice rough. "Nothing more."

"That can't be true," she said, reaching up to touch his face. "I have seen inside of you. There is more than this. He didn't destroy you. He didn't hollow you out. He only wins if you let him."

"You think it is so simple?" He wrapped his fingers around her wrist and pulled her hand away. "You think you can simply speak it and it will be true?"

"Why not? You think you can show me this, make analogies out of stone and sand and convince me that you were broken. That you are empty. That you are not the man who made vows to me. The man who read a book so he would know how to please me."

"No. It is impossible. Stop."

"What is impossible? What?"

"I cannot be more. I cannot give you more. I will leave you nothing but alone, and you don't want that. I will be everything you were hoping to avoid."

"You're wrong. You're wrong, because I wasn't looking to avoid anything when I came here. I was looking for anything, and it was all about me. It had nothing to do with you. I didn't think of who you might be at all. What you might come to mean to me."

"I am a killer. A machine. That is all. All I create is pain."

She grabbed hold of his hands, brought them to her cheeks and held them close to her skin. "With these hands? These hands that have brought me so much pleasure. And have been so tender with me." She smoothed her palms over his knuckles. "I know you have dealt out pain. I know you have been responsible for unimaginable destruction. In the pursuit of protecting your people. But when you touch me… I have never felt the way that I do when I'm with you. You are more. I've witnessed it. I've felt it."

He reached around, grabbing hold of her hair, holding her still, tethering them together. "I can't. I can't give more. I must keep focused. I must keep my eyes on my goal."

"Do you have to deny yourself forever?"

"Yes," he said.

"No." She leaned forward, battling against his grip, kissing him on the lips.

And he couldn't fight against this. Against the need that rose up inside him. The desire to be with her. He knew he was all wrong for her, knew that he could never give her what she wanted. Knew that he didn't possess the answers to the questions that were in her luminous blue eyes. But he wasn't strong enough to tell her no. Wasn't strong enough to turn away from this. Here, out in the desert where he had been the most isolated, he could not say no to this. To this chance to water the dry spaces inside him.

She had already compromised his control. And right now, facing down the desperation in her eyes, he didn't have it in him to try to reclaim it. He couldn't give her anything deeper than this. But if she wanted his body, he would gladly share it. And if she would share hers with him... He was not worthy. But he wasn't strong enough to say no. He had survived torture. Had been beaten, broken, had withstood terrible pain. But he could not withstand this desire. This desire that roared through him like a feral beast, tearing at everything in its path.

After this. After this he would rebuild himself. Would find himself again out in the desert as he had done once before. But not now. Now he would lose himself. In her. In this one way he had given himself permission to find release.

"There is a bed. Upstairs. It is not fine. It is likely full of sand."

She shook her head. "I don't care."

He lifted her up into his arms, held her close to his chest. Felt her heartbeat. She was so beautiful, so breakable. How was he entrusted to hold her in his arms? He was nothing. Nothing but a blunt instrument. Nothing but a weapon. What business did he have putting his hands on her body?

None. None at all. But he didn't possess enough honor to turn away from her, to turn away from this. He felt things breaking between them, splintering. Mirroring the broken pieces of humanity that were left inside him, buried deep. Shattered beyond repair. When she looked at him, it was easy to believe they might be fixed. Easy to believe that he could be whole. Because when she looked at him, she saw a man. But even if the pieces could be repaired, he knew for a fact there weren't enough left to ever create a whole man. Not in the way she deserved.

She saw more than he was. And he wasn't strong enough to end that illusion. Not now. After this it would have to end.

With each step he took, the sand depressed beneath his feet, another reminder of where they were. Of the fact that he was ready to strip this beautiful woman naked in the middle of the desert, in a house that was barely fit for a scorpion, much less a queen.

But even with guilt lashing at him, he couldn't stop. He wouldn't stop.

When they made it to the room he'd called his own for all those years, he set her down gently, her feet almost buried in sand. He went over to the crude metal bed frame and grabbed hold of the blankets, shaking them out fiercely. Now that he'd thought of scorpions, he had to be sure.

Her skin should never touch fabric this rough. Her body was worthy of only silk. And worthy of a man who knew better how to treat her. Better how to touch her.

Still, he walked toward her. Still, he wrapped his arm around her waist and tugged her against his body, kissing her deeply. Still, he brought her over to the bed and laid her down on the mattress. He was shaking as he let his hands drift over her curves, as he kissed her as if she was the oasis he'd been searching for.

Later. He would hate himself for this later.

He stripped her clothes from her, as quickly as possible, ruthlessly. No thought given to delicacy, to the expensive nature of her clothing. He heard fabric tear, and he didn't care. If he was more beast than man, he would prove it now. He had no idea if wanting a woman made every man behave this way, made even the most controlled, careful of men act without thought to consequence.

But he didn't care. It didn't matter what other men did. It didn't matter how sex usually felt. Because for him, this was unique. For him, this was the only experience. For him, there would be only her.

When she was bare before him, he bent his head and kissed the soft curve of her breast, drew her nipple deep into his mouth. Then he moved down lower, his tongue tracing a line down the center of her stomach. Her breath pitched, the sharp, sudden action an indicator of her pleasure. He knew. He was learning. She had been right. It didn't matter how much you knew about sex. You had to know about your partner. Had to care about them.

His hands followed the same journey his tongue had, sliding down her waist, gripping hold of her hips and around behind her, cupping her buttocks, lifting her gently from the bed as he buried his face between her thighs and tasted her in a way he'd become obsessed with in fantasy over the past week.

She cried out as he dragged his tongue over her slick flesh, focusing his attention on the bundle of nerves that was the source of her pleasure. He would happily die like this. With her flavor on his tongue, her soft sounds of pleasure filling the air.

She placed her fingers through his hair, tugging hard, and he took it as a sign to go harder, to go deeper. He had no refined skill; he had only desire. Intensity. A need for her that burned in his gut, that was physical pain.

He would never get enough of her. He could lose himself in her, in this. Could return back to this desert place as long as he had her with him. And it was no longer the kingdom he saw swimming before his vision when he thought of his purpose. It was glittering blue eyes, soft pink lips, blond hair his hands could get lost in. It was Olivia.

The realization hit him with the force of a thunderclap. Everything in him screamed its denial, but he pushed it aside. Because he didn't care for the future, not now, not with her slickness on his tongue, her desire coating his lips. He held more tightly to her, taking her against his mouth, lavishing attentions on her until she screamed, her voice echoing off the walls where there had before only been silence. This dry, barren place would never be the same again. Because it was filled with her.

And neither would he. Because he was filled with her, too.

He wanted her to be filled with him.

He shifted their positions, rising up to kiss her mouth, testing the entrance to her body with the head of his arousal. There were no preliminaries. He was not tentative as he'd been the first time. Rather, he thrust in deep on a growl, blinding white light flashing behind his eyelids.

He buried his face in her neck, relishing her scent, relishing her. Here he was, at the site of his desolation, in the place where he had been most isolated, most alone, as close to another person as one could possibly be.

He had no restraint now, no ability to hold himself back, and he gave thanks when she arched beneath him, crying out her release because it left him free to chase his own.

And when he did, he was consumed by it. Overcome as a lone traveler in a sandstorm, utterly devastated. Destroyed.

When it was finished, he had no strength left inside him. He could do nothing but pull her body against his and hold her as sleep took hold of him. There was no thought to anything else, no thought at all. Just the desire to rest.

That realization sent a jolt through him. Where had his focus gone? Was this moment of bliss the beginning of a road to ruin? Because it was difficult now to want anything but his own satisfaction. To lose himself in these sorts of moments. To weave a life together made of them. Of happiness and pleasure and comfort. Instead of purpose and loneliness.

But what will your people do if you lose your purpose? If you slide into corruption?

Just for a moment, he let himself imagine falling asleep with her. Making her his world. And a bright, intense burst of joy pierced the darkness inside him. A pure shaft of happiness like he'd never known before.

A happiness that scared him more than any pain he had yet endured.

It brought back memories. Memories long ago blocked out. His mother smiling. His father placing a heavy hand on his shoulder. Those words he could never hear.

Right then, he wanted to run. Right then, he wanted to get away. She made him remember. And that was even deadlier than forgetting.

CHAPTER TWELVE

"I LOVE YOU."

Olivia didn't mean to speak the words, but the moment they left her mouth she surrendered. Not just to the feeling, which she had come to terms with yesterday, but to the fact that she had just confessed it. She had said them many times over the course of her life. Her parents, to her sister. To her first husband. But never in all of her life had the response mattered so much. Never in her life had the words cost so much to speak.

Always, they had been the right things to say. A gift with nothing behind them.

But these three words spoken to him were like three strips taken from her hide. Essential parts of herself given to him because they were necessary. Because he was necessary. It made her vulnerable, she knew. It exposed every bit of the neediness she had been afraid of exposing all of her life. But she didn't care, not now. Because finally, finally she wanted something that was worth the cost. She wanted someone who was worth the cost.

Tarek was the strongest man she had ever known. If he could face down the pain, the fear that he had endured, the loss, then certainly she could give something of herself to him. Had anyone ever given themselves to him? She would.

She realized now that she had stopped giving of herself a long time ago. She was insulated, surrounded by people who kept walls erected between them. As she did, too. But she couldn't do that here. She couldn't do that now. Not with him.

She couldn't protect herself and love him. She would have to risk. Have to step out.

She had sworn she would never break. But for him she would have to. For him, she would break open and pour herself out. Show him her heart, her neediness, her everything.

For this man who saw her. This man who looked at her as if she was singular. Precious.

For this man, she would.

She felt Tarek stiffened beneath her hands. "Olivia, no."

"Yes." She knew already this would end badly.

That it would hurt like hell. But she was committed to it. She was so tired. She wanted to grab a sledgehammer and physically break something down to symbolize what she wanted to happen inside her. She didn't want protection or comfort. She didn't want safety. She wanted raw heat, passion. But the only way to get that was to walk through the fire. Better to burn alive than freeze to death.

"I cannot love," he said, his voice like stone.

"You can. There are a lot of things you didn't think you could do. I know you didn't think that you could make love to me…"

"Is that it? You are taking that as a sign of love? A sign of affection?" He moved away from her, standing by the edge of the bed, pacing like a caged animal. "I want nothing to do with love," he said, his tone fierce. "And even if I did, I lack the capacity."

She shook her head, feeling numb. "No. I don't believe that."

"Because of this?" He indicated the bed. "Any beast can rut. That does not indicate the ability to love."

"So now you're going to reduce this? Now you're going to make it nothing more than animals mating?"

"This was all about producing in heir, was it not?"

"Was it?" she asked, pain making her lash out. "If so, I hate to be the one to tell you, using your mouth on me, no matter how much fun it might be, will never produce an heir." Talking about a baby like this, a child, *their* child was suddenly a new, sharp pain. A sliver shoved beneath her skin, adding to the rest.

An heir was no longer a detached title, a strange, hazy goal. But a baby. Part her. Part Tarek.

A dream she hadn't realized she'd wanted so badly. One that was sifting through her fingers like sand with each angry word, each passing second.

His dark brows locked together. "I will not deny I derived enjoyment from it. But that is not an indication of finer feelings."

"What are you afraid of? What are you hiding from?"

"Hiding seems to be your game, my queen, not mine."

His words hit her with the full force of a slap. Because they were true. She was an expert at hiding. She preferred to hide among people, smiling, feigning connection, because it was a wonderful way to disguise the yawning ache of loneliness inside her. To pretend it was being satisfied. But she had admitted it to herself, so his words held no power. "Says the man who spent years hunkered down in this empty shell of a building?"

"I cannot keep my eyes on you and on my country. I have to remain focused."

"Life isn't that simple, Tarek."

"It got me this far."

"But there's more. Don't you want more? I want more. I'm tired of just getting by. I was protecting myself for so long. Accepting the blandest drop of human emotion because it meant I wouldn't have to give anything back. It meant I wouldn't have to risk anything. But when you don't risk anything, you get no reward. I ran all the way to Tahar from Alansund to avoid being alone. To avoid having to deal with the emptiness inside myself. I was willing to marry a stranger in order to keep from dealing with the fact that I just… My parents could never show that they loved me as much as they love Emily. And rather than admitting I needed it, that I missed anything I just kind of closed in on myself, made myself strong. I asked for more and found they were unwilling to give it, and so I stopped. I was married to a man I could barely go beyond small talk with because I would rather have a shell than lose the pretense we had. But it's not enough. I'm not going to let you get away with that. I'm going to ask for more than you think you can give. I'm going to demand it. If you were anyone else, I wouldn't care if you ever said that you loved me. If this were me two years ago, I would never demand it. But this isn't me two years ago. This is me now. This is me, being the woman that you helped me discover I am. So now you have to deal with it."

"And I am the stranger that you chose to marry. I am not now a man you can fashion into the image you would like to see. I am all you see before you. I am what I was made to be."

She got out of the bed, took a step toward him, bracketed his face with her hands. "Be more. You can be more than a goal. More than an ideal. Just because your brother was twisted, and evil, and completely beholden to all of his vices doesn't mean you have to be."

"You say that, and yet you know nothing of what I have seen. He killed my parents. Our parents. Our blood. He stopped just short of killing me because he thought I might be of some use, or perhaps because in his twisted mind he had power so he didn't need to destroy me completely. I will never know for certain. He said that he loved me. As he tortured me, he said that he loved me. *That* is love to me. Love is nothing more than pain."

She closed the distance between them, kissing him hard, not pausing to think her actions through. When she parted from him, they were both breathing hard. "Is that pain? Do you think I would cause you pain?"

"I think between the two of us we would cause nothing more than pain if we went down that road."

"It's too late. I'm down that road."

"Then, understand I will never meet you there."

His words sent a stab of pain straight through her, the kind of pain she had spent her life avoiding. She had laid herself bare to him, opened herself up, and he had rejected her. It was her deepest fear, and she was standing here in a hot, empty room, living it.

"I understand."

She understood, but she could not accept it. Not now. Not any longer.

"We must return now," he said. "We have a nation to rule. We can afford no more distractions."

Olivia knew there was much she could no longer afford. But it had nothing to do with the kingdom.

She had found the strength to love him. Now she would have to find the strength to walk away.

When they walked back into the palace, the antechamber was empty. Their footsteps echoed on the marble floor. Olivia had been silent on the drive back from the desert, but that didn't surprise Tarek. She was upset, but she would be fine. She had not come to Tahar for love. Had not married him for love. And so he had confidence she would survive the disappointment. And he would regroup. Rebuild. They would continue on as they had started. In that he was confident.

He would have to guard himself more closely, but he was able.

They didn't need love. She was wrong about love. Love was pain.

Love was only pain.

He began to walk deeper into the palace and sensed that Olivia was not walking with him.

He paused, and turned. "Olivia?"

"I'm leaving."

"What are you talking about?"

She shook her head. "I have to leave. I have to leave here. I have to leave you."

"Don't be foolish. You are not leaving me. You are my wife." He had never expected to have a wife. And now, he could not imagine his life without one. Without her. Pain wrenched through him, and he pushed it back.

"I know. And I married you before the entire country. I made vows to you. Promises. But I didn't know then what I wanted. I thought I could have a marriage like the one I'd had before. Where I asked for nothing, where I expected nothing in return. But that only works when I'm not really in love. You… I love you. And I need you to love me back. I deserve to be loved back."

A red haze fell over his vision, any control he'd laid claim to over the past fifteen years deserting him in that moment. He strode toward her, his heart thundering hard. "You think you can leave me? Have you forgotten who I am? Have you forgotten *what* I am?"

"It's you who have forgotten who you are. You've forgotten everything but the poison your brother put in your head. And I will not spend my life on the other side of your walls. I want more than that. I deserve more than that. You deserve more than that. Malik nearly destroyed Tahar with his indifference. And he tried to destroy you, too. But you would heal this country and never afford yourself the same. If they deserve it, your people, if this dust and rock you profess to love deserves it, why don't you deserve it?" She was shouting now, screaming at him. All of her pristine, contained manner gone. "Fight for this. Fight for us. Please."

"Wanting more leads to incredible acts of selfishness. As you are demonstrating right now."

"I'm not a human sacrifice to be thrown on an altar. Maybe you're right. Maybe this is selfish. Maybe I'm not being giving enough. But I would give you everything if you would let me. You just won't let me. And I can't…I can't pretend that I don't want more. I won't sit here and let you kill me by inches with your indifference."

"If there's one thing I'm not, it's indifferent. I want you. Isn't that enough?"

"It isn't enough. Because you don't want me. You want a body. You want a woman to stand at your side and be your queen. I want to be *loved*. I've spent too many years trying to fill that void with other things, trying to shut out the ache so I wouldn't be lonely. So I wouldn't hurt. But I would rather be lonely than lie to myself. I would rather hurt than hide."

He couldn't breathe. Felt as if he was being held down, subjected to a blade beneath his skin again. "Then, go," he said.

She blinked those blue eyes that hours ago he'd been thinking of as his horizon line. "What?"

"Get out. If you don't want this, then get out. There are plenty of women willing to marry a sheikh. I don't need to have an heir with you. If this won't make you happy, then leave. I will not hold you prisoner. You said you would never send me away. I made no such promises to you."

"And if there's a baby already?" she asked, tilting her chin up in the air.

"Then, we will handle it." His stomach tightened and he fought to maintain a streamlined hold on his emotions.

Anger was all he needed to feel now. There was no room for doubt, no room for hurt. "Now, get out."

"Tarek—"

"Get out!" he roared at her, not caring that she was undeserving of his rage. Not caring that he had brought this on himself. He was the sheikh. For the first time he would own that. For the first time he would take true command.

She didn't shrink; she didn't pale. Rather, she nodded her head slowly, as regal as the first moment he had seen her. Then she turned and walked out of the room.

Blinding, burning pain flashed through his chest, and he dropped to his knees.

Olivia was gone. Olivia was leaving him. The woman he'd never imagined he'd want. The woman who had become everything. She was gone.

And there was only pain.

Two hours later the car that was carrying his wife departed the palace. Tarek went to his room, locking the door behind him, pacing the length of the space, his heart pounding so hard he was sick with it.

He would not keep her here. He could not.

He also knew he could not hold her while clinging to his control. While keeping an eye on his goal. His people needed a leader who would cast aside all earthly pleasures, who would give of himself wholly. He could not do that while clinging to Olivia.

He stripped his clothes off, pacing awhile longer before lying down in his bed. He would sleep alone tonight. As he had every night. And as he would every night after.

He craved Olivia. There was no denying it. He was as weak as any man when it came to desire for a woman's body. A sobering realization. At least she was gone now and he would no longer be a slave to his needs.

He finally drifted into sleep, but it was restless, filled

with nightmares, ghosts of the past. Searing pain. Visions of the torture that had gone on within the palace walls. Visions that had been absent ever since Olivia had become a true part of his life.

He sat up, his torso drenched with sweat, shaking.

He swung his legs over the side of the bed, walked over to the window and looked out at the inky black desert. The moon was high in the sky, casting a pale glow on the sand. Such a desolate place, the desert. His kingdom.

It had seemed less so when she was here.

When she was here it was more like the years before Malik. More like when his parents had been alive.

Pain blasted him again, shooting through his skull. He didn't allow himself to have these memories, and his body accommodated him. Because it hurt too much. Because he loved her too much.

He thought of Malik, inflicting wound after wound on his body. All while promising love.

And he thought of Olivia, professing to love him. They were not the same things. How could they ever be? Because Olivia was nothing like Malik. His mother and father had been nothing like Malik.

His parents. He had so few memories of them. But they were there. Those twisted, broken shards of his humanity would never have existed in the first place if not for them. Back then, he had been whole. He had been loved. Not in the way that Malik had claimed to love him. It had been different.

He gritted his teeth against the pain of the memory. It was like trying to break through a brick wall. One he had erected. There was a very clear division in his mind. Life before the death of his parents, and life after. He did not allow his mind across the wall into life before because he did not like to remember. Because it split his focus from his purpose. Because it caused him nothing but pain.

Searing, unending pain. Much like the torture he had endured at his brother's hands.

Pain. At least in the desert there had been no pain. At least when he cut out every desire, every longing, every emotion, everything with a singular purpose before him, there could be no pain. And that was why it was so important.

Why it was so important to keep himself from wanting. Why it was so important to keep everything but that one goal stripped away. He had honed his existence into one of survival. Survival was simple. It cared not for comfort, for enjoyment. It cared only about breathing. Breathing was easy.

It was the rest that was difficult.

But he was not Malik. He had determined he would rule independent of his own desires. Was that not enough?

Unbidden, he saw a familiar face in his mind. Not Olivia's this time. His father's. And he heard his voice, soft, distant, from the unused recesses of his memory. The words. Those words he had longed to hear for so very long, muffled by pain and grief, now made clear.

I love this country. More than my own life. Without love, how can a ruler temper his power? What will he use as his guide?

A flood of memories filled him then, washing over the wall that remained, reducing it to rubble. Of everything that had happened before. Of who he had been before the torture. Before his exile. And he wished, more than anything, that he had Olivia here to hold him as the images overtook him. Brought him to his knees. Mingling with the grief he already felt over her loss.

He realized with sudden, stark clarity that whatever Malik had felt for anything, for anyone, it hadn't been love. He was the evidence of the absence of love and all the destruction it could cause.

What did it matter if he swore protection, if he professed loyalty in his speeches, if he gave of himself, if he gave his possessions, but there was nothing behind it? If none of those actions possessed love, what did they mean? And what could they become?

He saw now that love was not pain. Love was the very thing that kept a man rooted. No matter how fiercely he focused on his goal, if he felt nothing in his heart, there was no compass to guide him. No true north that would ensure his direction was true.

It was love that would see him making the compassionate choices. Love that would help him believe when everything was dark.

It was love that had helped him believe already when life was dark, even though he had been too blind to see it. The love of his parents.

Olivia had told him. She had told him that he was not what Malik had made him. Had insisted that he had been strong already, or he would have perished. She had been right. It was everything his parents had made him. Their strength. Their love.

Love was not the weakness. Love was the strength. Love was everything.

Olivia had shown him that, and he had told her to leave. He had been afraid. He had been holding on too tightly, but had no control. It was the fear. Fear of pain. That was what all of this had been. Him running. Him fleeing the kind of pain he had been subjected to in his past.

And now she was gone. Now was too late.

She was on a plane, back to Alansund.

She should run from him. She had been denied her entire life. Perhaps there was nothing more her parents could have done. Her sister had always been ill; she had said so. Whether or not they could have done better by her, they should have. Simply because she was Olivia. And she deserved the best of everything.

She most certainly deserved a man who wasn't shattered inside. Most certainly deserved a man who chose to love her the first time she asked.

Not a man with scars both inside and out. Not a man who had wounded her, told her to leave. Not the man who could scarcely imagine coming after her because he had never been away from his country, never been on a plane.

She was his queen. The queen he wanted ruling beside him. The queen of his heart.

Her kiss had changed him back from stone. Had demolished the walls inside him.

She had given him a new goal. Love. And with it, facets to his existence. More than simple survival. More than breathing.

He had no idea what he brought to her. No idea what he had done to deserve the feelings she claimed to have for him.

But if she would have him, he would claim her.

It didn't matter how impossible it seemed to leave. Didn't matter how far he had to go to find her. He was more when he was with her. He was the ruler he needed to be. He was a man.

And that meant whatever it took, he would see it done.

Olivia had never felt such pain. This truly was losing a part of herself. A grief so strange, so open-ended, she didn't know what to do with it. It wasn't like losing someone to death. There was no reclaiming someone who was gone. But Tarek was still walking around on this earth, and she could not have him. Could not be with him.

She had never loved like this before, either. With all of herself. Unreservedly. She had made herself vulnerable, and she was paying for it. Yet again she was paying for demanding more.

But she wouldn't go back, either.

She realized now that though it was Emily who'd been sick all of her life, Olivia had allowed herself to be crippled inside. To shut her emotions, her desires, away so she wouldn't suffer more rejection.

But now she had.

And she felt more alive than ever. She had been so afraid of loving with all of herself. Because it would leave her vulnerable. Leave her exposed. Marcus's loss had only seemed to confirm that. But as badly as it had hurt, she could only be thankful at the time that she hadn't given him her whole heart. Because she'd been afraid long before that loss.

She hadn't taken any medication for the flight back. She'd been too lost in her sadness over Tarek to feel any anxiety. More than that, she wasn't afraid to show it if she did. That was half of why she'd taken the pills. Because she was more afraid of showing her fear than of not being able to cope with it.

She didn't care now. She supposed that was one thing.

She felt battered, broken. But strong. Because she had endured now, hadn't she? Had faced down her deepest fear, returned alone, back to this palace, useless. No place for her.

But she didn't care. Didn't care that she wasn't useful. Didn't care if she was underfoot. Didn't care to make herself indispensable so that someone might deign to care that she was around.

She loved Tarek. No matter what he did. No matter what he said to her, no matter how useful he was.

Didn't she deserve the same?

She felt she did.

Too bad most of her wanted to get back on a plane and

beg Tarek to take her back, whether he ever loved her or not. There was a very large part of her that felt pride was overrated in this situation.

It isn't about pride. Pride is nothing. It's about wanting to live.

She knew what life was without love. She'd spent her entire life closed off to it. Desperately wanting it, and denying herself because she was so afraid that others would hold it back from her. Now that she had truly felt it, she didn't want to go back. She couldn't.

There was a sharp knock on her bedroom door, and she peeled herself off her bed, smoothing her hands over her hair. "Yes?"

"My queen." She heard her lady's maid Eloise on the other side of the door. "There is a man here to see you. He says…he says he's your husband."

Her heart stopped, everything in her freezing.

"That's impossible," she said.

That was when Tarek chose to stride into the room. It had been only two days since she'd seen him. But she felt very much—and she knew it was desperately corny—as if he was an oasis in the middle of her emotional desert. The first sight of water and shade she'd had in a long crawl across burning sand.

He was so tall, impossibly strong and broad. His face so beautiful. The sharp, defining angles, those lips that could be both soft and commanding depending on how he chose to wield them.

He was a powerful enemy to those who opposed him, wonderful with the sword, she was certain. But as far as she was concerned, his body and all that he could make her feel with it was his most powerful weapon.

"I did not tell you that you could come in yet," Eloise said, clearly full of pique.

"I did not ask. I am the Sheikh of Tahar, and I am

Sheikha Olivia al-Khalij's husband. It is my right to see her. More than that, it is my due."

Olivia shivered, her new title, her new last name, somehow erotic and intensely affecting on his lips. "It's okay, Eloise. Leave us."

Eloise very clearly didn't think it was okay. However, she obeyed Olivia's command.

"I have never been on a plane before. I can't say I enjoyed it," Tarek said.

"Flying is terrible. I hate it. Why are you here?"

"I came here to get you, you foolish woman."

Her heart scampered up into her throat. "I told you. I can't live with you in a one-sided relationship. I just can't. For so many reasons."

"You said you needed to be loved."

Her throat tightened around her heart, strangling her. "I do. I hate to try to explain what it was like to be married to Marcus. Because in many ways I hate to compare the two of you, because you're so different. Because what I feel for you is so different. Also, Marcus is dead and I can ask no more of him. He didn't do anything wrong. He didn't disappoint me. He didn't deny me. But I didn't love him. Not like I love you. It was easy to be with him. We never had to know each other. Neither of us were interested in sharing or being shared with. It gave me companionship without having to make myself vulnerable. Without putting my feelings in any danger. Which you... I can't do that with you. I want all of you. I want to open myself up and make you understand me. I want you to open yourself up to me. You make me so unbearably aware of how isolated I've been. And now that I know, I can't go back to that."

He closed the distance between them, cupping her cheek, his dark eyes blazing into hers. "I cannot go back. I can't go back, either, nor do I want to. I was so alone. I stripped away every desire. Every emotion. Because I so desperately didn't want to remember. I so desperately didn't want to feel pain." He laced his fingers through her hair, his eyes never leaving hers. "We are so much the same, Olivia. And when you first walked into my throne room I never would have thought so. But we were both protecting ourselves. I tried to protect myself to the end. I blamed love, because somehow I understood it had the power to devastate the most. It was easy to focus in on my torture, on the pain. On all the hate. Because then I could pretend it was the most painful part of what I had been through. It wasn't. It was the loss of my parents. The loss of their love. And I wouldn't even let myself remember it, because I wanted nothing to do with the pain. And so I rid myself of every emotion. I focused solely on my goal. So that I could survive." He shook his head. "And then you came. You made me desire. You made me want. You did exactly what you've accused me of doing to you. You opened me up. Demolished the walls. And I was frightened. But after you left I realized that love was never the enemy. Yes, it hurts. It has the power to devastate. I was devastated by the loss of you." He swallowed hard, his Adam's apple bobbing up and down. "I remembered my parents. Remembered words my father said to me. That hurt, too. But there was so much good in it. I realize now that you can't have the good things without the pain. I was all right with that for a long time. But I'm not now."

"What did you remember about your father?" she asked, her throat aching.

"That he loved Tahar. That he loved my mother. That he loved us. And I know for a fact Malik loved none of those things. If he loved any one thing, it was himself. It is the absence of love that hurts. That wounds beyond repair. If there is no love, every action is empty." He pressed his forehead against hers. "I am tired of being empty."

"You aren't. You never were. Being with you... Seeing your strength... It's what made me find mine."

Tarek looked down at the woman he was privileged enough to call his wife. And he could no longer hold back the words that were bursting to be released from him like a torrent of water. He had used his words so sparingly over the years. Preserving them as though they were precious things. Perhaps he had saved them for such a time as this. Perhaps he had saved them for her.

Those things he'd hoarded inside him. His splintered humanity, the things that made him human... Perhaps they had all been saved for her. She made him feel as though he might not be splintered at all.

She made him feel as if he was whole.

"When I speak of love, I speak of love in general. But it is not love in the general sense that made me realize this. It was my love for you." He pressed a kiss to her temple, everything inside of him shaking. "I love you, Olivia."

He felt her sag in his arms, her whole body trembling. "Oh, Tarek. I love you, too. I love you, too. I'm so glad you love me."

"Love is powerful. We have good reason to fear it," he said, smoothing her hair. "Like any weapon, you must wield it well. And then it is an asset. Even if it is still dangerous."

"That makes sense. Since I first met you, you told me you were a weapon."

"And you told me you were a genteel, cultured queen. You did not tell me that you were, in fact, much more deadly than I."

A smile curved her lips. "I didn't know."

He recalled the first time he had seen her. He had thought her frail. A white lily who would dry quickly in the harsh desert heat. But she had not been changed by the desert. Rather, the desert had been changed by her. He had been changed.

"Be my wife, Olivia," he said, his voice rough.

"I already am."

"You became my wife for politics. Stay my wife for love. When I ask you now, I ask you for no other reason than that I cannot live without you. I have lived without a great many things, but I could never survive without you."

She drew a shaking breath, and pressed a kiss to his lips. "I will be your wife."

"Do you remember, that first day, you told me you needed to be with me because there was no other place for you?"

"I remember," she said, her words a whisper.

"You have made a place in my heart. And you will always have it. I swear this to you."

A tear rolled down her cheek, a smile tugging at her lips. "More vows?"

"Yes. And I may yet make more. I'm new at this after all."

"So am I. But that's okay. We can learn together."

EPILOGUE

TAREK DID MAKE more vows to Olivia. He made several every night, often while he was lost in her body. He never could get enough of being so close to her. Of being so connected, so loved, when he had spent so many years alone.

With her, he relished a great many things he had forgotten to want. Soft beds, good food. Birthday cakes that were never thrown away, and always shared together. Smiling. Olivia gave him so many reasons to smile. And less than a year after they were married she gave him yet one more.

Olivia walked into their shared bedchamber. They had not spent one night apart since he had come to get her in Alansund all those months ago. And, not coincidentally, he no longer had nightmares. There were no more ghosts in the halls of the palace. They had all been laid to rest by her.

"I have some news for you," she said, her tone serene. But he was not fooled, because it was the same tone she had used when she had first come to the palace and proposed a marriage agreement between them. It was the tone she often used when she was about to broach something quite monumental and was trying to catch him off guard.

So strange to know another person so well. So wonderful.

"Unless you have invaded Germany, I imagine we can deal with it."

"No," she said, waving her hand, "no invasions today. However, I have been to see the doctor."

"Have you?"

"It seems that you are finally going to get your heir." And that was where her serene front ended. Tears welled in her eyes, and a smile broke out across her face. "But more important than that, we're going to have a baby."

Tarek took his wife into his arms, pressing a kiss to her lips, and then everywhere else he could reach.

She laughed. "I take it you're happy?"

He was a man who had spent many years believing he was stone. A man who had resigned himself to spending life alone. And in his arms he held the most beautiful woman in the entire world, who had just told him she was going to give birth to a baby. His baby.

He was suddenly so full, he could scarcely breathe.

"I did not know such happiness existed until you," he said, kissing her again.

She closed her eyes and breathed in deep, as though she was relishing him. No one had ever relished him before. No one except for her. "Neither did I, Tarek. Neither did I."

* * * * *

#3373 SEDUCING HIS ENEMY'S DAUGHTER
by Annie West

Donato Salazar's plan to jilt his enemy's daughter is the ultimate revenge and beautiful Ella Sanderson is certainly sweet enough! But as their fake wedding day approaches, one question weighs heavily on Donato's mind: to love, honor...and betray?

#3374 HIDDEN IN THE SHEIKH'S HAREM
by Michelle Conder

When Prince Zachim Darkhan escapes capture he takes the daughter of his nemesis with him. But while Farah Hajjar is hidden in his harem the line between hatred and desire soon blurs, leading Zachim past the point of no return.

#3375 THE RETURN OF ANTONIDES
by Anne McAllister

Widow Holly Halloran's fresh start is only a plane ride away, until Lukas Antonides—the man she wishes she could forget—strides arrogantly back into her life. As tension mounts between them, so too does that bubbling attraction of old...

#3376 RESISTING THE SICILIAN PLAYBOY
by Amanda Cinelli

Leo Valente is as notorious as the tabloids say he is. But feisty wedding planner Dara Devlin isn't deterred. She needs his family castle for her top client, so she boldly accepts Leo's outrageous challenge to be his fake girlfriend!

YOU CAN FIND MORE INFORMATION ON UPCOMING HARLEQUIN® TITLES, FREE EXCERPTS AND MORE AT WWW.HARLEQUIN.COM.

HPCNM0915RB

REQUEST YOUR FREE BOOKS!

HARLEQUIN

Presents®

2 FREE NOVELS PLUS
2 FREE GIFTS!

PASSION GUARANTEED SEDUCTION

YES! Please send me 2 FREE Harlequin Presents® novels and my 2 FREE gifts (gifts are worth about $10). After receiving them, if I don't wish to receive any more books, I can return the shipping statement marked "cancel." If I don't cancel, I will receive 6 brand-new novels every month and be billed just $4.30 per book in the U.S. or $5.24 per book in Canada. That's a saving of at least 13% off the cover price! It's quite a bargain! Shipping and handling is just 50¢ per book in the U.S. and 75¢ per book in Canada.* I understand that accepting the 2 free books and gifts places me under no obligation to buy anything. I can always return a shipment and cancel at any time. Even if I never buy another book, the two free books and gifts are mine to keep forever.

106/306 HDN GHRP

Name	(PLEASE PRINT)
Address	Apt. #
City	State/Prov. Zip/Postal Code

Signature (if under 18, a parent or guardian must sign)

Mail to the Reader Service:
IN U.S.A.: P.O. Box 1867, Buffalo, NY 14240-1867
IN CANADA: P.O. Box 609, Fort Erie, Ontario L2A 5X3

**Are you a current subscriber to Harlequin Presents® books
and want to receive the larger-print edition?
Call 1-800-873-8635 or visit www.ReaderService.com.**

* Terms and prices subject to change without notice. Prices do not include applicable taxes. Sales tax applicable in N.Y. Canadian residents will be charged applicable taxes. Offer not valid in Quebec. This offer is limited to one order per household. Not valid for current subscribers to Harlequin Presents books. All orders subject to credit approval. Credit or debit balances in a customer's account(s) may be offset by any other outstanding balance owed by or to the customer. Please allow 4 to 6 weeks for delivery. Offer available while quantities last.

Your Privacy—The Reader Service is committed to protecting your privacy. Our Privacy Policy is available online at www.ReaderService.com or upon request from the Reader Service.

We make a portion of our mailing list available to reputable third parties that offer products we believe may interest you. If you prefer that we not exchange your name with third parties, or if you wish to clarify or modify your communication preferences, please visit us at www.ReaderService.com/consumerschoice or write to us at Reader Service Preference Service, P.O. Box 9062, Buffalo, NY 14240-9062. Include your complete name and address.

HP15

SPECIAL EXCERPT FROM

❧ HARLEQUIN

Presents®

Read on for a sneak preview of
RESISTING THE SICILIAN PLAYBOY,
the first book by So You Think You Can Write winner
Amanda Cinelli.

"Are you asking me to pose as your date?"

"What other reason would we have for being in Palermo together? I think it's the most believable scenario, don't you?"

Maybe it was tiredness after the past twenty-four hours catching up with her, but Dara felt a wave of hysterical laughter threatening to bubble up to the surface. The thought that anyone would believe a man like Leo Valente was dating a plain Irish nobody like her was absolutely ludicrous.

He continued, oblivious to her stunned reaction. "You would leave the business talk to me. All I'd need is for you to act as a buffer of sorts—play on your history with his family. Someone with a personal connection to smooth the way."

"A buffer? That sounds so flattering…" she muttered.

"You would get all the benefits of being my companion, being a guest at an exclusive event. It would be enjoyable, I believe."

"Umberto Lucchesi is a powerful man. He must have good reason not to trust you," she mused. "I'm not quite sure I can risk my reputation."

"I'm a powerful man, Dara. You climbed up a building to get a meeting with me. I'm offering you an opportunity to get exactly what you want. It's up to you if you take it or not."

The limo came to a stop. Dara looked out at the hotel's dull gray exterior, trying desperately to get a handle on the situation. He was essentially offering her the *castello* on a silver platter. All she had to do was play a part until he got his meeting and she would be done.

"What happens if you're wrong? If having a buffer makes no difference?"

"Let me worry about that. My offer is simple. Come with me to Palermo and I will sign your event contract for the castle."

She thought about the risk of trusting him. He hadn't given her any reason to trust him so far. But what other possible reason could he have for asking her to go with him?

A man like him could have any woman he wanted, so it wasn't simply attraction—she was sure of that.

He obviously wanted in on the Lucchesi deal very badly if it had prompted him to consider her event. His reaction earlier had been a complete contrast, his refusal so clear. It was a risk to lie to a man like Umberto Lucchesi, but on the scale of things it was more of a white lie. And the alternative meant losing the contract. Losing everything she had worked for.

"If I go with you—" she said it quickly, before she could change her mind "—I want a contract for the *castello* up front."

Leo felt triumph course through him as he felt Dara's shift toward accepting his offer. He'd seen the uncertainty on her face, knew the difficult position he was placing her in.

"You don't trust me, Dara?"

"Not even a little bit."

Don't miss
RESISTING THE SICILIAN PLAYBOY
by Amanda Cinelli,
available October 2015 wherever
Harlequin Presents® books and ebooks are sold.

www.Harlequin.com

HARLEQUIN

Presents®

Suave, sensual and utterly scandalous...

Leo Valente is as notorious as the tabloids say he is. But feisty wedding planner Dara Devlin isn't deterred. She needs his family castle for her top client, so she boldly accepts Leo's outrageous challenge to be his fake girlfriend!

✂

SAVE $1.00

on the purchase of RESISTING THE SICILIAN PLAYBOY by Amanda Cinelli {available Sept. 15, 2015} or any other Harlequin Presents book.

Redeemable at participating outlets in the U.S. and Canada only. Not redeemable at Barnes and Noble stores. Limit one coupon per customer.

52612754

5 65373 00076 2 (8100)0 12069

COUPON EXPIRES OCT. 19, 2015

Available wherever books are sold, including most bookstores, supermarkets, drugstores and discount stores.

www.Harlequin.com

HARLEQUIN
Presents®

A fabulous story of alchemy, desire and an exiled king returning to power from *USA TODAY* bestselling author Abby Green

From the essence of desire…a king's baby!

Exiled King Alix Saint Croix is in need of a little distraction while he waits to reclaim his throne! Stunningly exotic perfumer Leila Verughese has everything he needs in a *mistress*. After only one night he finds she has everything he needs in a *royal wife*. Bride sorted, throne nearly there! There's just one problem—Leila's refusal, and the fact that she's already carrying his heir…

Find out what happens next in:

HEIR FIT FOR A KING
October 2015

Stay Connected:

www.Harlequin.com

www.IHeartPresents.com

f /HarlequinBooks

🐦 @HarlequinBooks

P /HarlequinBooks

HPI3375